ALL RISKS

Mike Lowe

FEEDAREAD
www.feedaread.com

Published in 2019 by Feedaread Publishing
Arts Council Funded

Copyright © Mike Lowe

First Edition

The author asserts the moral right under the Copyright, Designs and Patents Act 1988 to be identified as the author of this work.

All Rights reserved. No part of this publication may be reproduced, stored in a retrieval system, or transmitted in any form or by any means without the prior written consent of the publisher, nor be otherwise circulated in any form of binding or cover other than that in which it is published and without a similar condition being imposed on the subsequent purchaser.

A CIP catalogue record for this title
is available from the British Library

ALL RISKS

For David, my editor, with grateful thanks

Also by Mike Lowe
Milvar's Path
Paul Thomas adventures: Going Dutch and Banger
Hermit
LoGO
All at Sea

1

Philip Harding squeezed further into the corner by the door of the underground train as more people crammed onto the compartment. He was travelling later than usual and had hit the rush hour.

No more than five foot six tall, his face was crushed against the rucksack of an Australian back-packer and the young man's heel had pinned Philip's foot to the floor. Philip could tell the man was Australian because the flag sown onto the flap of his rucksack was an inch from his eye and he could see the individual stitches that made up the stars of the Southern Cross quite clearly.

An hour earlier and the train from Baker Street to Kings Cross would have had empty seats and he could have sat back in comfort watching the people and wondering about their lives and loves. He could have looked out for the girl who usually travelled at that time and fantasised about her.

But David Maltby, the Managing Director of the United and Overseas Insurance Company had kept back several of the senior staff to offer them the chance to transfer to the company's new branch in Peterborough. It would mean promotion for Philip and it would mean he didn't have to make the journey from Letchworth to London every day. Maltby had told the people it affected to think about it over the weekend. If they decided to accept the change they would be moving at the beginning of September – not four months away.

The Australian stepped back even further as more people added to the crush by the doors, anxious to be first out when the train stopped. The heel of his boot scraped painfully down Philip's shin. Philip gave the big Ozzie a shove and freed his trapped foot. He would have to fight his way out of the train before a fresh lot getting on at Great Portland Street pushed him further into the carriage. That had happened before, and he hadn't been able to get out until the next stop.

Philip struggled into a position where he could make a determined push for the doors as soon as they opened at the station serving both Kings Cross and St. Pancras.

There were so many people getting out behind him that he was carried along by the sheer weight of numbers, his feet not landing firmly on the platform until several feet from the train. He went with the flow along the platform and out onto the escalator.

At the top he managed to step to one side for a moment to catch his breath. As he headed for the mainline station he was debating whether to go to the bookshop and buy a magazine when he thought he saw his fantasy girl out of the corner of his eye. When he turned around she was nowhere in sight, yet he was certain it had been her. He had been watching out forher for some weeks, ever since she had stood close beside him on the train. He had been able to look closely at her without embarrassment as there was nowhere else to look. They h ad not actually made eye contact, but he was able to admire her brown eyes. She had very fair hair which he felt sure was natural, pulled into a little bunch at the back; she was tiny, about five foot two, but as he was short himself that was perfect. He guessed she was in her early twenties, she wore little or no make up, no jewellery and no perfume that he could discern. She didn't dress smartly. She always seemed to be carrying a large folder or portfolio and he guessed she might be an art student. If he caught sight of her it made his day. He promised himself that if he ever managed to get close enough again he would speak, and maybe even ask her out. He realised with a slight shock that if he moved to Peterborough he would not see her again and he would miss her.

There she was again, he was sure it was her, even though he could only see her back. She was wearing a simple pale-yellow summer dress and her comfortable flat shoes enabled her to walk quickly; he walked faster to keep her in sight. When she stopped near the WHSmiths bookshop to speak to a man in a business suit, Philip hung back and pretended to consult a time-table. He saw the girl hand the portfolio to the man and in return receive an envelope or maybe a package, which she put it into her shoulder bag before turning towards the exit. A black cab drew up at the rank and she got in. As the taxi drove off he caught a glimpse of her fair hair as the light from the station entrance caught it. He was very tempted to hail a taxi himself and say, 'follow that cab,' but instead he turned back towards the platform where the train would take him home to Letchworth.

It had been raining at some stage in the train's journey and there was an unpleasant musty smell of damp dust coming from the seats. Philip felt empty, bereft almost, the girl had been so close, and now she was gone. The carriage filled up and became more uncomfortable, but Philip barely noticed his travelling companions. He could think of nothing else but the blonde girl, all the way back to Letchworth.

All weekend, Philip tried to concentrate on the new opportunity that he had been offered; a new job in a brand-new branch, his own department maybe, more money, less travelling, a new start in fact, a chance to make his mark. But he couldn't concentrate, all he could think of was the blonde girl.

After lunch on Sunday he half-heartedly scanned the many sections of the *Sunday Times* then threw it down and sighed.

'What's up with you, moping about like a wet weekend. Why don't you get yourself out and have a good time?' Walter, Philip's father asked. 'I'm sick of seeing you hanging round the house. You make it look untidy.'

'Why don't you go out yourself, I don't feel like it,' Philip snapped, 'I've got a lot to think about.'

Philip's mother had died when he was a boy and he had been brought up by his father, who still treated him like a child. The family had lived in Harrogate where Philip had gone straight from school to work in the insurance company. When he had been transferred to the head office in London, his father had suggested moving south where they could share a house nearer to Philip's work.

London was too expensive, so they had opted for Letchworth, a pleasant town, less than an hour's train journey from London. It had worked well enough to begin with but now, at thirty-two, Philip felt stifled and would have liked an excuse to get out and find a place of his own but dreaded his father's reaction to such a suggestion.

'What have you got to think about, you never do anything or go anywhere, it's time you found yourself a young woman. I shall never have any grandchildren at this rate. You *do* like women, don't you?'

'Well as a matter of fact I have got a girl, she lives in London and I'm thinking of moving in with her.' Philip blurted out. 'Trouble is I've been offered a job in Peterborough and I have to decide what to do.'

'Oh, you didn't tell me, what's her name? When are you going to bring her home for me to see?' His father's eyes sparkled at the thought. Philip regretted the lie immediately.

'We'll have to see, just leave it for now will you,' he replied sharply.

Walter had been retired some years and had few interests. All he did was potter in the garden and watch racing on the television. That and giving unwanted advice to Philip on all aspects of his life.

Philip decided that he must speak to the blonde girl somehow; if she didn't want to know, he would just move to Peterborough and forget her, but if she responded to him and accepted his invitation to go out, he would stay in London, for the time being at least. He had always regarded the move to London as temporary and longed to return to the north where he could breathe good clean air. He had made very few friends since moving to the head office in London and his work colleagues all seemed to have interests that excluded him; they talked about what they were going to do at weekends and although sometimes he would have liked to join in, they never invited him.

There were few opportunities to indulge in his love of outdoor pursuits apart from holiday times when he still liked to meet up with friends in Yorkshire to go walking, rock climbing or sailing. But he was good at his job, his bosses thought the world of him; he got results and was meticulously accurate and conscientious. He would never leave a job unfinished even if it meant staying late in the office. Hence the Peterborough job offer. He would be a fool to turn it down; he hated the train journey from Letchworth every day, he would be able to buy a house of his own in Peterborough and get away from his father. He would have preferred a posting further north, back to Harrogate preferably, but Peterborough would be a start.

'Mr Maltby wants to see you straight away, Mr Harding, in his office,' the pretty receptionist called to Philip as he entered the foyer of the company's impressive head office in Baker Street. He nodded and made for the executive lift that would take him to the top floor and his boss's penthouse suite of offices.

He was going to have to decide about the new job. He had not slept well all weekend for thinking about it. Of course he wanted the job, who wouldn't, it was a marvellous opportunity. But he kept thinking about the blonde girl. 'You're a fool, just forget her,' he told himself as the lift climbed to the seventh floor. 'You can't give up this job on the off-chance some girl might agree to go out with you. The chances are she'll refuse anyway, even if you can pluck up courage to ask her. Now snap out of it, go in there and tell him.'

He hoped he hadn't been talking out loud; old Maltby had probably got the lift bugged. He allowed himself a smile at the thought, checked his tie was straight in the lift's mirror and stepped out of the lift into the sumptuously appointed foyer to the executive suite.

Maltby's secretary must have been chosen for her looks, all she did was smile and ask your name. She had a computer and a telephone switchboard on her desk, but everyone knew that Maltby used the general office on the lower floors for all his correspondence.

'Morning, Mr Harding,' she purred, 'Mr. Maltby is expecting you, just go on in. Would you like coffee?'

'Oh, yes, please, Angela, that would be nice.'

'Harding, dear boy!' exclaimed Maltby, getting up from his leather chair and making the journey round his huge desk to greet Philip. The desk, adorned only by a telephone and a silver framed photograph of Maltby's wife, put Philip in mind of an aircraft carrier. The office was furnished like a gentleman's club, with bookcases filled with leather bound books from floor to ceiling. Strategically placed table lamps gave the room a pleasant cosy feel and lit the gilt framed portraits intriguingly.

'How are you? Come and sit over here,' the big man indicated the easy chairs grouped round a coffee table beside a window overlooking the city. Philip walked over, his feet sinking into the deep pile carpet. He shook hands and allowed himself to be escorted to a chair. From his seat he could see the bustling street below, with its glass fronted buildings and one of Wren's churches, the name of which he didn't know, looking somewhat incongruous among all the straight lines. Not a sound from the traffic reached the top floor of the building and there was an air of surreal calm.

Neither man said anything while Angela fussed around them with coffee cups and plates of chocolate biscuits.

'Thank you, Angela, my dear; we'll be all right now.'

Both men watched appreciatively as the young woman walked to the door and closed it behind her.

Maltby stirred sugar into his coffee and sipped it before setting the cup down. Selecting a chocolate biscuit, he waved to Philip, indicating that he should do likewise. It was not until Philip had his coffee-cup and a biscuit in his hand that Maltby spoke.

'Now, you know why I've called you in, Philip, you've had all the weekend to think about it, but I dare say you could have told me on Friday, eh? We shall need to talk through some details of course. It's basically as I said to the others but what I am offering you is branch manager. You've made excellent progress in your time here at head office and you're ready for promotion. You are more than ready for it, in fact you've earned it since you came down to us from the frozen north,' he laughed at the joke he always made about the company's Yorkshire branch. 'The offices in the centre of Peterborough are brand new and very prestigious, the company has high hopes for expansion in that part of the country and once it is established it will be our regional head office. Now, I hinted at the salary, didn't I? I don't think you'll be disappointed with the package. It comes with a top dollar motor as well of course, you can choose pretty much any make of car you like, Simpkins will give you all the stuff on that, I can't remember the details. You've impressed the board over the years my boy and now you get your reward.'

Philip was overwhelmed, Branch Manager, he hadn't expected that, had he heard correctly? Maltby seemed thrilled to be making this offer. His eyes shone, and his face was flushed, his huge grin showed glints of gold.

'I don't know what to say, Mr Maltby,' he began.

'David, please, you're management now, call me David, I insist.'

'Oh, well, David, I don't know what to say. I am flattered of course and, well, of course I'm delighted. You won't be disappointed in me.'

'I know that, my boy, I know that, we have every confidence in you. Now you must bring your good lady one weekend and spend some time with us at the house, get to know each other a little bit you know, Fiona is looking forward to meeting you.'

'I don't have a lady-friend just now I'm afraid, sort of in between if you know what I mean,' Philip began, fumbling for words.

'Oh, I understand, say no more, don't worry about it, you'll soon find yourself another young lady, very important you know, to have the right lady on your arm when we meet up with the big names.' Maltby leaned forward, patted Philip's arm and smiled.

Philip had met Maltby's wife, Fiona, a couple of times at office functions but of course she wouldn't remember him. She was like all the women in Maltby's life, beautiful, expensive, but not very bright.

The thought of spending time at 'The House' as Maltby called his sprawling mansion in Berkshire, appalled Philip, but he just smiled back with what he hoped was a man-of-the-world smile.

'I'll look forward to it, David.'

'Right oh, then. Talk to Simpkins on your way down and I'll see you during the week to talk about staffing for the new branch,' He stood up, a sure indication that the interview was at an end. Philip got to his feet and moved towards the door. Maltby joined him and opened the door for him.

'Have a good day,' Maltby said, already thinking about his next appointment as he dismissed Philip and headed back towards his huge desk.

'That's that then,' Philip thought to himself as he rode down to the second floor in the executive lift. 'You've done it; you're the new branch manager.' He felt slightly dazed. He had no idea at all what was involved, or who would be going with him. Would Maltby expect him to appoint staff? It was bewildering.

He went into his office and sat at his desk, staring unseeing at the pictures on the wall. Then he remembered he was supposed to have seen Alan Simpkins on the way down. Simpkins was the personnel manager and very friendly with Maltby. He and his wife often spent time at 'The House'.

He would be the man to talk to in order to find out more about his new job. He made for the lift once more. Several people called out, 'Congratulations, Harding' and, 'Well done!' as he walked through the open-plan part of the office. How did everyone know already?

'Hello, Harding! Well done, come on in,' said Simpkins as Philip entered his office, 'you've seen the old man, I take it. Everything OK?'

Alan Simpkins was one of the 'old school' types that Maltby liked to have around him; very smartly dressed and sporting an RAF tie. He was a decent sort but not someone with whom you would make idle conversation.

'Well, yes, OK, I guess. Thanks, by the way. I haven't got much idea what Maltby was saying. I gather I have been offered manager of the Peterborough branch, I haven't been asked to formally apply for it or anything. Do you have any details?'

'Oh yes, it's all been approved by the board and everything, contracts and so on have been drawn up, I've got them here, I shall need you to read through them and sign of course but take your time. Here,' he said, handing Philip a hefty folder, 'I have put together a dossier of all the information about the new office, the other senior staff will have to confirm their acceptance of course, that will be done today I expect but you should find everything you need here. Anything else you want to know, just ask me.'

'Oh thanks, that's great, I felt a bit as if I had stepped off a cliff when I left Maltby. I was wondering what would happen when I hit the ground.'

'If I'm to believe what I've heard about you, Philip, you'll hit the ground running. Don't worry about a thing, everything will be fine.' Simpkins laughed and shook Philip's hand.

'Well thanks, you are very reassuring,' mumbled Philip glancing through the contents of the folder.

'Oh! I nearly forgot – your car!' beamed Simpkins, picking up another folder from his desk. 'You'll see in there what your options are, but if you have any particular preferences I'm sure we'll be able to accommodate them. Most managers seem to favour Mercs, but they are a bit staid I always feel. Have a think about it, OK?' He stood up and opened the door for Philip and again shook his hand as he left.

Philip couldn't believe this was happening to him, 'branch manager, top job, top salary, posh car, 'wow!', he said quietly to himself as he headed for the lift again.

He rode the lift down to his floor and his feet hardly seemed to touch the ground the whole way. Back in his office he took out the contents of the folders and spread them out over his desk, sorting them into piles and studying each one in turn. The remuneration package, pension, health insurance and company car, a big wadge of stuff about the duties of a branch manager; the setting up of accounts, transfer of some existing customers to the new branch and more. Simpkins seemed to have done a very thorough job and everything Philip needed to know was there.

He began to feel a little more confident. After all, he told himself, he did know pretty much all there was to know about the business; he had established himself as an authority on certain types of insurance when he was in the Harrogate branch, so much so that several senior members of staff often consulted him. He sat back in his chair when he had examined the entire file. 'Yes,' he said with conviction, 'I can do it!'

'What was that, Mr Harding?' said Julie, his secretary, as she walked into the office with a tray of coffee and biscuits.

'Oh! Sorry, Julie, nothing, I think I must have been talking to myself. Have you heard my news?'

'Yes, I have, congratulations! I am so pleased for you.' She put down the tray and poured his coffee, added brown sugar and milk and stirred vigorously. 'There you are,' she said. 'Was there anything you wanted me to do?'

'No, thank you, Julie, not just now. That will be all. Have you got things to do?'

'Oh yes, I have plenty of work, but if there is anything you need I can leave it . . .' She hesitated a moment before leaving, closing the door behind her. Philip glanced again at the pile of paper on his desk and picked up the information about cars.

He had never thought of himself as a motorist, although he had learned to drive as soon as he was old enough to have a licence and had enjoyed driving the old cars he had been able to afford. As he travelled to work each day by train and used either the tube or taxis for business in London there was no need even to own a car, but when he moved to Peterborough he guessed a car would be very useful and he warmed to the idea of something prestigious. He pressed the intercom button.

'Yes, Mr Harding?' came Julie's reply.

'Would you come in please? – As a matter of fact, there is something you can help me with,' he said, as Julie entered the office. 'What sort of cars do you like?'

'Cars, Mr Harding? What do you mean?'

'Well I have to choose a new company car, it goes with my job you see, but I don't know what to have. Any ideas?'

'I like Jaguars myself, we could never afford one of course. My Gary has an old Rover and I've got a Mini, but given the choice I would have a Jaguar, they're lovely!'

'Would you like to come and help me chose one?'

'Ooh, would I? Yes of course, gosh how exciting,' she twittered and agreed to meet Philip in the foyer at lunch-time when they would and have a look round some showrooms. Philip thought dealers for all the top makes were fairly close, in Mayfair and in Park Lane.

Philip had never said more than a couple of words to Julie apart from work topics and he was surprised how easy it had been to invite her to help him. He hadn't really taken a great deal of notice of Julie, she was just someone who was always there, taking dictation, opening and sorting mail and making coffee. Philip looked at her now, her eyes shining with enthusiasm for the task ahead. She had seemed so keen too. Perhaps if he took the bull by the horns and asked his dream girl she would accept as readily. He still doubted himself but vowed to try to meet the girl somehow.

Philip was glad to have Julie with him as they browsed among the shiny monsters at Stratstone's, the Jaguar dealer in Mayfair. She held onto his arm and looked for all the world as if she was his girl. He enjoyed the experience as much as looking at the cars.

'Good afternoon, Sir, Madam. Is there anything I can help you with? Do you have a particular model in mind or do you need advice?' The salesman smiled with a small bow in deference to his customers' money.

'I'm not sure, I fancy a Jag, you know, but they seem so big,' began Philip. The salesman opened the door of a large saloon and gestured to Philip to get in. Allow me Sir. The seats are adjustable, as you see. Madam, would you like to get in the passenger seat?' Once they were installed the salesman crouched down beside Philip and began explaining the benefits of Jaguar ownership, pointing out some of the finer points of the car's considerable specification. 'You can have any colour you like of course, I'll get the colour chart for you. Leather is standard on this model but if you preferred we could do cloth upholstery. Now, does the lady drive? You see the seat can be programmed to your own setting so that all you have to do is flip a switch and the seat automatically sets itself to your preferred height and reach. I can arrange a test drive sir, if you would care to give me your card, I can arrange for a car to brought round to your office for you.'

'That would be good, but I'm not sure this is the model for me, let me look at some others,' interrupted Philip.

A little while later and out on the street again, Philip and Julie were laughing. 'That was close, we almost finished up with one each!' said Philip, holding on to both of Julie's hands.

'I know, they are a bit keen aren't they. But they are lovely cars, don't you think?' said Julie, evidently enjoying herself.

'Oh, without a doubt, but I'm not sure I can see myself in a great big thing like that, I'm only little you know.'

'Oh no, you are a big man now, Mr Harding, very important, you must have an impressive car,' she laughed.

'Oh, please call me Philip, Julie; even the boss calls me Philip now.'

'All right then, Philip. I will. Now if you think the Jaguar was too big, what about a Porsche?'

'Oh yes, that's a good idea, I think they have a showroom in Park Lane. It's not far to walk.'

Without even thinking about getting back to the office they went from showroom to showroom all afternoon, even looking at Ferraris and Aston Martins.

In the end Philip had had enough of cars but had enjoyed himself more than he had for years. Julie had been good company, so easy to talk to and laugh with. It was getting late and he told her she needn't go back to office, he would see her in the morning.

Philip did go back to the office, but everyone had gone home so he picked up his briefcase and bade the doorman goodnight.

2

There was so much to do before the move that time flew by. Half of Philip's time was spent in the new offices in Peterborough, supervising the installation of computer systems and furniture, interviewing staff and making contact with local business people prior to the big opening.

Julie had accompanied Philip on many of the trips to Peterborough and they had been getting on very well.

'Julie,' began Philip, one morning, when there was a lull in activity while they waited for a computer engineer to sort out a problem with one of the PCs, 'had you given any thought to transferring to Peterborough yourself?'

'Well, as nothing had been said, I guessed I hadn't been considered for the move,' she said, 'but if there was a chance of me moving it would be good because we live in North London, Palmers Green you know, and although it would be further, it would be easier to get to work than going into the city every day. It would suit my Gary, too, as his job has him travelling all over East Anglia.'

'Oh, well in that case, if you would like to move, I would like you to continue to be my secretary. It will mean more work and sometimes longer hours, but it would also mean a salary increase. I hadn't realised they had left it to me to appoint my own secretary and of course nothing has been said because I had done nothing about it.'

'Ooh, that's super, Philip, I would love to carry on being your secretary. I hope I'll be able to do the work though, it will be different I expect.'

'Not for you. You'll be meeting more clients and there'll be some business lunches and stuff like that, but the day to day stuff won't be a lot different. You'll come then?'

'Yes!'

'Good, then that's settled. I'll inform personnel.'

For some weeks Philip had not been catching the underground train on which his fantasy girl usually travelled because he'd either been working later in the London office or in the new office in Peterborough, but today he'd left the office early, and there she was, standing by the door, holding onto the rail with one hand and clutching her portfolio with the other. She had on a pair of faded jeans and an overlarge navy-blue sweater against the evening chill that made her look even smaller than usual, she hadn't tied her hair back, and it looked very natural, with a slight curl. Philip felt an overwhelming desire to give her a big hug.

There was already a crush by the doors, but Philip contrived to squeeze in right beside the girl and when the train lurched she was thrown against him, just as he hoped she would be.

'Oh, I'm sorry, did I step on your foot?' said the girl, looking up at him.

'No, it's OK, really, couldn't be helped.'

Go on, say something else, he urged himself, quick before it's too late. 'I, I think I've seen you on this train before, and we've bumped into each other before.' He had to get her talking somehow.

'Oh really,' said the girl, pleasantly, looking up at him again. 'Come to think of it, yes I think I have seen you; weren't we squashed together once, I remember being a bit embarrassed at the time,' she laughed. 'Do you usually travel at this time then?'

'Not always, but I do if I can, to miss the worst of the crowds at Kings Cross. Where are you headed?'

'I'm going to Kings Cross, too.'

'Do you fancy a coffee or something, when we get there?' said Philip, hardly believing he had managed to speak.

'Well I have to meet someone there . . .'

'Oh, I'm sorry, I just thought,' he mumbled awkwardly.

'Oh, but I won't be long, I could have a coffee with you after I've seen him, if you like.'

Philip couldn't believe his ears. 'That would be great, shall I wait for you then, at the coffee shop, or would you prefer something alcoholic?'

'No, that's OK, come with me, I just have to give this to my colleague and then I'm free, won't take more than a minute or two.' She smiled, and Philip melted.

They got off the train at Kings Cross and Philip had to struggle to keep up with the girl as she threaded herself through the crowds. He thought for a moment she might have been trying to lose him, having said she would have a coffee to humour him, but no, as he emerged from a thick crush of people, there she was, waiting for him. She smiled and set off again. He guessed she would be meeting the man at the same place he'd seen the exchange before but couldn't risk losing sight of her. He was slightly out of breath by the time they reached the mainline station bookshop. The man in the suit was waiting, they exchanged packages and she was at Philip's side.

'OK, all done. Let's have coffee!'

They found a table in the corner, away from the crush. Feeling he must be dreaming, Philip sat gazing at the girl as he sipped his coffee. He was unaware of the jostling crowds all around them.

'Are you OK?' she said peering into his eyes and waving her hand in front of his face. 'You look as if you are dreaming.'

'I think maybe I am. Listen, you'll think I'm crazy, but I have been longing to speak to you for ages and now I am with you I can't think what to say. I'm sorry. What is your name? I'm Philip.

'I'm Andrea, but most people call me Andi. Don't apologise, I'm flattered. Why didn't you speak before? I don't bite.'

'I know that now, but you seemed so, I don't know, unreal somehow, and I'm a bit shy.'

'Tell me about yourself, Philip, what do you do?'

After telling Andi a little about his job, Philip discovered that Andi was not a student but an artist, working in an art studio attached to a gallery off Edgware Road, mainly doing repairs and restorations to paintings and other works of art. She also made copies of paintings for collectors to hang in their houses while the valuable originals were safely stored in bank vaults. She sometimes had to deliver items to customers and that was what she had been doing today.

Andi was very lively, bubbly and giggly, easy to talk to and unsophisticated, her face was very expressive, and she used her hands a lot when talking. Philip was captivated; she laughed every time she caught him staring at her.

'You are funny, Philip, it's almost as if you had never spoken to a girl before,' said Andi one day after he had said something she thought rather soppy. Then she looked hard at him as if reading his mind, 'You haven't have you, you aren't used to girls at all!' She laughed and threw her arms around him. 'But you are a dear!'

They contrived to meet every day Philip was in London; Andi took him to lots of art galleries, teaching him about painting and sculpture. They ate in back street restaurants that he would never have ventured into on his own. After a few months Philip had learned enough about art to enable him to enjoy it more than he had thought possible, he could talk to Andi about paintings without feeling ignorant. They also went to concerts and although Philip was already very keen on classical music, Andi had introduced him to types of music he had never heard before. They got on extremely well, tending to like the same things and laughing a lot.

On the days he had to go to Peterborough, Philip couldn't concentrate on what he was doing. Even his new friendship with Julie failed to distract him. It was nearly the end of July and he was trying to think how he would explain to Andi that he would be moving away from London. Peterborough is not that far of course, he argued with himself, he could come down to

London at weekends to see her. He didn't know where she lived, she had avoided answering when he had asked, perhaps she lived in north London somewhere and it would be easy to meet, perhaps even in the evenings as well as weekends. He was convinced it would be all right. He would explain next time her saw her.

Andi took the news of the move very calmly; in fact, she seemed pleased that Philip was doing so well.

'Peterborough is not far, I'll come and see you there sometimes and you can come to London to see me other times,' she said, smiling. Philip laughed and had to explain that he had argued the very same thing to himself but had not dared hope she would see it that way.

'Why ever wouldn't I? Of course I am pleased. We'll still see each other, won't we?'

'Of course, yes, of course we will!' He hugged her and twirled her round. 'This calls for a celebration, what shall we do?'

For the next few months, during which the arrangements for the move took a lot of Philip's time, and then after the actual move for several more months, they had not been able to meet very often but they had spoken on the phone most days. On the occasions they were able to get together they made the most of the opportunity and always did something special.

Late in November they had arranged to meet in town after Philip had been to a meeting at head office, they went to a show in the West End and then to a restaurant. Over the meal Andi told him she was worried about something and needed to talk to him about it.

She had told him a lot about her work and the restorations she did, often for some of the big galleries. Recently there had been a painting that as far as she was concerned was a good copy of a Manet, showing a riverside scene. She had done a lot of work to the painting which had been badly damaged. She hadn't known who the painting belonged to, and she had forgotten it until she was browsing through the catalogue of one of the auction houses and had seen the original Manet offered for sale. At first, she thought it was a coincidence that the original had turned up so soon after she had worked on the copy and, because she had taken an interest in the painting while she worked on it she thought it would be good to see the real thing. She went the sale-room and asked to see the picture. She knew immediately she saw it that this was the painting she had worked on.

'How could you be so sure?' asked Philip, 'if it was a good copy it would be just like the original wouldn't it?'

'It's impossible to make an exact copy, and anyway I had got to know that painting very well indeed, I know it was the one I worked on and I know it was not an original. Philip, there is something dodgy going on.' She looked at him steadily and he could see that she was serious and that she was in no doubt whatever.

'Have there been any other occasions when you have suspected anything untoward?'

'Well I hadn't thought so until then, but I thought about other paintings I had seen in the gallery, some I had worked on and some that had just gone straight out again, nothing I could say for sure, but because they were very valuable paintings or were by particular artists I liked, I had studied them. Some I was actually commissioned to copy, as I said, so that the owners could safely show off their paintings while the originals were locked away. I remember thinking it was strange that so many well-known paintings had suddenly come in for minor repairs and then been offered for sale.'

'You think they were copies as well?'

'I don't know, you see, unless you are an expert it is very difficult to tell, I'm not an expert but I do know my Manet, I have studied him, and I reckon I can spot a dodgy one. The others could have been fakes too, and now I think about it I wonder. You see in a small gallery like ours, good paintings don't come in very often, but as I said, a lot came up over a short period of time.'

'What sort of period of time are you talking about?'

'Oh just a few weeks – no, a few months, I suppose.'

'And you don't know what happened to the paintings?'

'No, I don't often go to the sales, it's too frustrating seeing things I would like, being sold to people who just want them as investments.'

'Is there any way you could find out where they went, who bought them or which sale-rooms they went to?'

'It would be difficult, but there must be records somewhere, I could try to find out. Do you think it sounds like fraud, Philip? It has been worrying me. I feel better for having told you about it.'

'It does sound very suspicious. It would be interesting to find out more about it. Do you think the copies you made might have been passed off as originals?'

'Oh, no, I don't think so. An expert would be able to spot one of mine, I'm sure. Although, I suppose they might get through in a small auction house.'

In the ensuing weeks Philip thought very little about the paintings because he was so busy at work; it was just a few months after taking on the new job in Peterborough, but he was feeling ten years older. He had even noticed a few grey hairs at his temples and his face was drawn and pale. He had managed to get the new branch up and running and everything was going well, with new business targets not only met but for some types of business handsomely exceeded.

When at last Philip had a weekend free, he phoned Andi to suggest they meet.

'Oh, Philip, thank goodness you've called. I'm so worried.'

'Why, whatever is it?'

'I can't tell you over the phone, I'm at work. I'll see you at the usual place – say seven o'clock. Is that too early?'

'No, of course, that's perfect. I'll come straight from the office. Are you going to be OK until then?'

'Yes, I guess. See you soon. Bye.'

Philip was worried. Andi had seemed very distressed and he could only guess it was something to do with the paintings. He hoped she hadn't got mixed up in anything.

3

As might have been expected, the train was late and so it was well past seven when he arrived at the little restaurant in Soho that they had made their own.

'Mr Harding! How are you? We are getting worried. Miss Andi is here waiting. Go on through, I bring you drinks.' Takis, the big Greek proprietor gestured to the back of the restaurant where, in the dim candlelight, Philip could see Andi, sitting at a table in a corner from where she had sight of the door.

'Oh, Philip!' Andi gasped, getting to her feet and running to meet him, 'I thought you weren't coming. Are you all right?'

'I'm fine; the train was late, snow on the line or something. I'm so sorry. But what about you? What is the matter?'

'Let's have a drink first and then I'll tell you.'

'Bring us a bottle of white makedonikos please, not too cold,' Philip called to the proprietor, who was hovering by the bar.

Takis brought the wine and poured two glasses before disappearing again, ready to be summoned when needed.

'Now, tell me,' pleaded Philip when they had both sipped a little of the fresh white wine. 'What is troubling you?'

'I told you I was worried about something dodgy going on with the paintings, well it has gone a big step further. I've been asked to copy a painting.'

'But isn't that what you were doing anyway?'

'Yes, as you know I have made copies for people to display instead of the original which is kept locked up somewhere, but mainly I was just touching up and repairing paintings. I have also done copies for my own amusement, and I think perhaps someone must have found out, or maybe seen one or two of my efforts.'

'But the people for whom you have made copies wouldn't tell anyone that their painting was a copy would they? And you haven't shown them to anyone?'

'No, of course not. I think my flat has been broken into.'

'What? Have you told the police? When was this?'

'No, I haven't told the police. It was a couple of weeks ago, and I wasn't sure at first. I just felt that things were not as I had left them. It was just a feeling. Nothing was missing, at least I didn't think anything was taken. Then a week ago I was tidying up my little studio – of course it's just a bedroom really – but it's where I paint, so I call it a studio. Some of my paintings are stacked up against the wall waiting to be framed if I decide they are good enough, and I'm almost sure there was one of my early attempts at a copy among them, but it wasn't there. I've looked everywhere, and I can't find it. Then just a day or so ago. No, I know when it was – it was Wednesday, I'll never forget it, a man came into work and spoke to the boss who then came over to me and said the man wanted to talk to me. He said could we talk outside and I looked to the boss who nodded, as if to say it was OK. Well, we went out to the corridor and this man, he didn't give me his name, said he wanted to put a proposition to me. He wanted me to paint a copy of a Manet. I thought at first he was just another collector and it was OK. But then he asked if I could make a copy that was so good it could not be distinguished from the original. Well, that is very difficult indeed and most of the copies that are made for collectors would not fool anyone who knows what to look for, but the collectors are happy to have something that looks near enough like the real thing. This was something else, why would he want a painting that was indistinguishable from the original?' Andi paused for breath and took a sip of wine, looking at Philip for his reaction.

'So, what did you say?'

'I said I didn't think I could do it. But the man said he was sure I could. He would make it worth my while. By now I was beginning to put two and two together and felt sure that someone had seen my paintings. They knew I could make copies almost like the real thing.'

'But you wouldn't do that would you? Not if you thought they were planning to pass the painting off as genuine?'

'No! Of course not. I hate the whole art forgery business. I told the man I didn't want to have anything to do with it. He told me to think about it and he would contact me again. He left, and I asked my boss who the man was. He wouldn't say but warned me to be careful.'

'Is that all he said? Be careful?'

'Yes, I asked him to explain but he wouldn't. I'm worried.'

'Had you seen this man before? What was his name?'

'No, I had never seen him before and he didn't tell me his name.'

'Could you describe him?'

'I could do better than that, I could draw him!'

'That's great, do that then, because if we go to the police with this, it will be an enormous help.'

'But I am not sure about going to the police . . .'

'Never mind about that now. The painting that you said was missing. What was it?'

'Oh, it was nothing very spectacular, just a small A.J.Casson. I like his stuff and I just thought it would be nice to have one of my own on the wall.'

'I've never heard of A.J.Casson, is he very valuable?'

'Quite. I couldn't afford to buy one. Most of his oils go for around twenty or twenty-five thousand pounds but bigger ones up to eighty or ninety.'

'Wow, worth trying to forge then?'

'I would think so, yes.'

'Do you think these people, whoever they are, might try to sell your copy?'

'They might, but the big auction houses would spot it straight away. Apart from the fact that it is a quite well-known painting, it isn't good enough to fool an expert. At least I don't think it is.'

'Just supposing they did want to try to sell it – how would they go about it?'

'Small gallery somewhere in the Midlands perhaps. Not London, I don't think.'

Philip sat back in his chair looking at Andi. He smiled.

'What are we going to do, Philip? Don't just sit there looking goofy.'

'I'm sorry.'

'Listen Philip, this is serious and I'm very worried. Are you going to help me?'

'Of course I am. I don't know how though.'

'I would like to get away from London for a while, somewhere the man can't find me. Can I come and stay with you in Peterborough?'

'That's a good idea. Yes, I've got a big house with plenty of space. You can move in any time you like.'

'I don't mean I want to move in with you, exactly, Philip,' Andi hesitated, 'You know what I mean – not yet anyway.'

'No, of course, no strings attached. You can have your own room and everything.'

'That would be lovely. When could I come?'

'As soon as you like. We can go this evening if you like. Let's eat first then you can collect some clothes and stuff and we'll get the last train. It goes at about eleven thirty I think.'

'Oh, thank you Philip. I am sorry to be a nuisance.'

'You couldn't be a nuisance if you tried. Now what do you fancy to eat? Takis!'

'Yes, Mr Harding, Miss. Here is menu. We have nice Keftedakia. You would like?'

'Have you got kalamarakia?'

'Yes of course, with horiatiki salata?'

'That sounds good. What about you, Andi?'

'I'll have the meat balls I think. Thank you, Takis.'

Takis went away and was back a moment or two later to ask if they wanted any more wine.

'No, we have to be on our way soon, Takis, so we'll manage with what we've got. Thanks.'

They didn't speak while they were waiting for their food, Andi still going over in her mind the events of recent days and Philip wondering how on earth he could help her.

The food was, as usual, wonderful, but they didn't do it justice. Andi just picked at her meatballs and Philip left most of his salad.

'Oh, my goodness, what is wrong?' exclaimed Takis when he saw their dirty plates. If anything wrong we will give another dish on house.'

'No, Takis, it was lovely, we are not hungry this evening. Please tell chef it was very good.'

It was just after ten when they left the restaurant. They took a taxi to Andi's flat in Camden, where she packed a holdall full of clothes. They then took another taxi to Kings Cross.

Consulting the departures board, they saw that the last train was due to leave at eleven five, they still had plenty of time.

'The bar is still open, we could have a drink if you like,' suggested Philip.

They sipped their drinks in silence. Andi was thinking about the implications of living in Philip's house. She was very fond of Philip but was not sure how much closer she wanted to get just yet. Would he assume –? 'Oh, dear', she thought, 'is it a good idea?'

Philip was thinking how nice it would be to have Andi living in his house. He could see her whenever he wanted, not just weekends when they managed to be together for just a few hours. His thoughts raced ahead, and he felt excited.

The station had a different atmosphere late at night. There were fewer people about and they didn't seem to have the urgent need get somewhere in a hurry as people had earlier in the day.

A man with a very wide brush was walking up and down, sweeping up a day's worth of discarded rubbish. When he got to the end he gathered up the rubbish and deposited it in a bin attached to a little trolley. Then off he went again, no hurry, lost in thought no doubt. It was the sort of job that allowed one to think. Philip and Andi watched him for a while, then turned to each other and smiled.

They checked the departures display again and headed for their platform where the train waited. There were very few people on the train and they were able to choose where to sit.

They chose seats with a table and sat facing each other. Neither seemed inclined to talk.

When at last the whistle blew and the train began to move, Philip said, 'We're off.' Ever since he was a little boy he had enjoyed the moment the train began to move and it was difficult to tell if his train was moving forwards or the train alongside was moving backwards. His father had always said, 'We're off!' and Philip always said it to himself. Now he could say it aloud. He smiled.

'What is it, Philip, what are you thinking?' asked Andi when she saw him smile.

Philip explained, but Andi was not in the mood for such things. She looked at Philip, a small man, about five foot six, neatly dressed, quite nice looking, she thought—a slight wave in his brown hair, cut in a very conservative way. Shy, yet very successful in business. Just shy with girls perhaps. He had not had much contact with women. His mother had died when he was young, and his father had brought him up. It struck her that she wanted to mother him. The thought made her smile, and Philip noticed.

'My turn to ask you what you were thinking.'

Rather than answer, Andi got up and went around to Philip's side of the table and sat close to Philip, who put his arm around her shoulders. She snuggled closer.

'That's nice,' said Philip, 'I'm going to like having you in my house.'

4

The house Philip had bought, a modernised Victorian building in one of the Orton villages just outside Peterborough, was far too big for a single man, but he thought it would be useful for staff functions and for entertaining important clients. Andi was thrilled with the house and the room Philip said she could call her own. It had an en-suite and even its own stairs down to what had at one time been the servants' entrance, way back in the Victorian era when the house had been home to a large family. She could be as independent as she pleased.

'It's lovely, Philip, really. I absolutely love it. I've never had such a nice room in my life before!' Andi enthused as she came downstairs. She threw herself at Philip and hugged him tight, burying her face in his shoulder. She stayed like that for a while until Philip eased her away so he could see her face.

'You're crying!' he exclaimed.

'Don't you see, Philip, I feel safe now. Thank you so much.' She hugged him tight again and would not let go.

'I'm going to look after you now. You don't have a thing to worry about. Nobody knows you are here.

Peterborough is a nice place, you can explore at your leisure.' Philip pulled her from his shoulder again and kissed her gently, still holding on to her. 'Shall we have a cup of tea or something?'

'Oh, yes, that would be nice. I'll do it, where is the kitchen?

Philip led Andi by the hand, through the sitting room, past the library, and his study and into the spacious kitchen where he showed Andi the cupboards in which tea and coffee were kept.

'Gosh, my whole flat would fit into this kitchen. Why do you have such a big house, Philip?'

'I know, it does seem a bit daft, but I thought it would be useful for entertaining.'

'But you'll need a staff to keep this lot going. You'll be like a squire!' Andy laughed delightedly as she boiled the kettle and prepared tea.

They sat in the kitchen drinking their tea and munching biscuits in comfortable silence for some minutes before Philip spoke again.

'I have the weekend free, what do you say we explore the city, show you the sights, have a meal out, enjoy ourselves.'

'Sounds wonderful. But let's just sit here for a bit first. I like it here.'

Later, after Andi had explored the rest of the house and made herself comfortable in her room, they went into the city and after looking at shops, finished up at the cathedral.

They spent quite a long time marvelling at the Norman architecture, still essentially the same as when it was built in the thirteenth century, and the wonderful wooden ceiling, the only one in England and only one of four in the world dating from that time. They learned from a guide that Oliver Cromwell had destroyed the stained-glass windows and the library.

They were able to forget for a little while Andi's problems and were feeling much happier after they had eaten in a city centre pub and returned to Philip's house.

Philip had been wondering about introducing Andi to his father. Walter Harding had been very unhappy at Philip's decision to set up on his own and the two had not spoken since Philip moved to Peterborough. Taking Andi to see him would please the old man and it would be a good way to make amends.

'I would like to take you to meet my father, Andi, would you mind?' Philip asked tentatively.

'No, of course not. Where does he live?'

'He's still in Letchworth, it's not far. How about we go tomorrow?'

Walter greeted Andi with open arms, his eyes twinkled as he gave her a kiss on the cheek.

I didn't think you really had a young lady, you know, when you told me, but I am delighted you have. I might have some grand children yet'

'Dad!' exclaimed Philip. 'Don't embarrass the poor girl. We've not known each other long.'

'Well, you don't want to waste any time, you're not getting any younger.' He chuckled mischievously.

To Philip's immense relief, Andi joined with Walter's laughter, saying it was OK.

Philip had wanted to throw a party, a sort of house-warming-cum-Christmas-cum-thank-you to the staff of the new office who had all worked so hard to make it a success. Julie had offered to organise it and had done most of the preparations.

Philip had invited Maltby but was relieved when the big man said he would just look in.

'It's your do, old chap, a chance for you to be magnanimous for once; you don't want the boss stealing your thunder. Fiona and I will be delighted just to pop in and have a drink, then we'll make an excuse and leave you to it. Splendid idea of yours to throw a party by the way. Well done!'

Philip had thought long and hard about whether it was appropriate to invite Andi to the party. People knew about her of course, you can't hide a pretty young woman for long, but she was not his wife or his fiancée and this was intended as a party for the staff.

'Of course you must invite her, Philip!' exclaimed Julie when she asked him what was troubling him.

'Do you think so?'

'Of course I do, you can't leave the poor girl out of half of your life.'

Andi was not sure about going to the party, but Philip managed to persuade her. She insisted on going to the West End to buy a dress. She said she didn't want to show him up.

Philip was not happy about her going back to London, but she explained that she would need to go to the city to find a suitable dress, and the chances of bumping into the paintings people were remote, so off she went.

5

The party was a great success, everyone had taken trouble to dress up for the occasion and all of Julie's preparations had paid off. There was dancing to a good five-piece band in the marquee in the garden and the champagne flowed freely all night. Philip made a point of talking to all the staff and their partners and was pleased that it was all going so well.

Philip had also, somewhat reluctantly, invited his father to the party. He was ashamed to admit that he feared his father would let him down, but he could not invite his girlfriend and not his father, so he invited him, hoping the old man would not want to come to a party with lots of young people. But he did, he dressed suitably for the occasion and could be seen in the centre of a small group telling his tales of life 'in the good old days'.

Philip was however disappointed that Andi had, after all decided not to come. He had sent a car to pick her up, but it had returned empty.

'No answer, Guv',' the driver had said.

'Did you check the studio?'

'Checked all round, Guv. Everything was in darkness.'

Philip had phoned, and Julie had phoned but there was no reply. He did his best to enjoy the party but despite the best efforts of Julie and his closest associates he couldn't take his mind off Andi. She had seemed keen when he saw her off the day before, although it had taken him some time to convince her that she could hold her own in any company if she put her mind to it.

At about one o'clock, the members of the band had packed up their instruments and been given supper before departing in their Transit van.

Taxis had been arriving at intervals to take guests home, and just as the last group of guests had departed, the telephone rang, and Philip rushed to pick it up.

'Hello.'

'My name is Darren Wilson, I'm a friend of Andi Pertell, I don't expect she's mentioned me to you, I've known Andi for ages . . .'

'Oh! I'm sorry, look, I didn't know,' began Philip, taken aback.

'No, it's OK, really. You don't understand, I'm not blaming you for stealing her from me or anything, we weren't, we're just kind of buddies, you know. But . . . '

'But what?' asked Philip, who was wondering what this was all about.'

'Well, I'm very fond of Andi and I look out for her. She told me about the paintings and that she was going to be staying with you, and I thought that was a good idea, but then when I phoned she told me she was going to some party and was coming back to London to buy clothes, so I went round to her place, to see if I could persuade her not to go to the party, not because I didn't approve of her being with you or anything but . . .'

'Will you please get to the point,' said Philip, getting more impatient.

'I'm trying; just bear with me will you. You see, Andi had told me about you and everything, and I thought it would be good for her to have some nice friends and that, but I was worried about how she would cope like, with all these business people, and I didn't want her to be embarrassed and that. So I thought it would be better if she didn't go.'

'Oh, I see, well she didn't come after all,' interrupted Philip, sharply, 'So thank you for interfering!'

'No, I know, well at least I guessed, you see, oh, this is difficult. You see . . .'

'Yes, and?' said Philip getting exasperated with the man.

'Well, what I'm trying to say is, she wasn't at her flat when I got there, but she hadn't gone to the party either, so I didn't know what to do.'

'Well if she wasn't there, you must have thought she *had* gone to the party; what are you getting at?'

'The new dress she'd bought specially was on her bed, all ready to get into, and her shoes and other things were all laid out, so she obviously hadn't gone to the party, but I can't find her. I wondered if you'd heard from her, or anything.' The words "or anything" struck Philip in the solar plexus. He said nothing for a moment, just stared at the telephone handset as if it had bitten him.

'Are you there?' Darren was saying, over and over again.

'Yes, yes, I'm here, look, I expect Andi has told you where I live, I can't leave just now, so can you come. We need to talk.'

'Oh, all right, yes, I suppose I can. It'll probably take getting on for a couple of hours to get there.'

Philip paced up and down in the hallway, waiting for Darren to arrive. He could think of nothing but Andi and this new development – a close friend of Andi's who had tried to persuade her not to come to the party. Why would he do that if he was not a rival for her affection? He had implied not, but Philip didn't think a platonic friendship was very likely.

Julie came out of the kitchen where she had been stacking dirty dishes and glasses in the dishwasher, she saw Philip and realised something was very wrong. She went up to him, took his hand and looked into his eyes.

'Phil? Whatever is it?'

'Huh?'

'What is the matter; are you still worried about Andi? I expect she just had second thoughts, maybe felt she wouldn't fit in.'

'That's what Darren said. No, she would've been OK. I don't think she had second thoughts. Something has happened to her.' He looked at Julie and she felt as if he was looking right through her.

'Who's Darren? Why do you say that, I'm sure it'll be all right, you'll see,' Julie said, and tried to give him a reassuring hug, but he shrugged her off.

'No, it won't be OK. Darren is one of her friends, he just rang. She's disappeared.'

'How do you mean, disappeared? I don't understand. Please tell me what has happened.' Julie took Philip's hand and led him to a seat in the living room and sat him down.

'Let me get you a drink, or a cup of tea or coffee, yes, that's what you need, a cup of coffee, stay there,' she said, all in a rush, and disappeared back into the kitchen. A moment later, Maureen from accounts, who had been helping Julie with the catering, came out of the kitchen, she was a motherly type, about sixty and quite bonny. She sat beside Philip and put her arm around his shoulders, something that, in normal circumstances, she would never have dreamed of doing.

'There dear, it'll be all right I expect, don't go worrying about it, we'll find out what has happened.' But Philip was in a daze and didn't respond. After a few minutes Julie came out with a cup of coffee, Maureen took it from her and offered it to Philip.

When the doorbell rang some time later, Philip became alert again and jumped up, walking quickly to the door.

'Hi, there, are you Philip? Oh, right, I can see you are, I'm Darren, I phoned . . .'

'Yes, I know, come in, come in,' said Philip, ushering him inside. Darren was thirtyish, stocky, about five foot seven or eight, with dark unruly hair and an ill-kempt beard. He had on a canvas jacket and paint spotted jeans.

Julie and Maureen watched in amazement as Philip led the man through to the living room. 'Get Darren a drink would you,' said Philip to no-one in particular. 'What'll you have?'

'Oh, not for me thanks, I'm off the drink, a cup of tea would be nice though, if there's any going.' Julie and Maureen returned to the kitchen to get the tea and discuss this development.

Philip and Darren spent some time talking while Julie and Maureen hovered, not knowing quite what they should do, but Philip called them over and tried to explain what seemed to have happened. He was so distressed that it was difficult to understand what he was saying. Darren kept interrupting with his own interpretation. Philip's father hovered at the edge of the group, not understanding what was being said.

Julie and Maureen gathered that Darren was a friend and associate of Andi's and that they worked together as artists. Darren had continued to keep an eye on Andi even after Philip came on the scene and he was always at her beck and call. He used to see her almost every day until she had moved up to Peterborough, and then phoned her most days to see if she was all right.

When Andi had gone back to London to buy clothes for the party, she had phoned Darren to tell him all about it.

Once they were all up to date with the situation as Darren saw it, they sat in silence, nobody knowing what to say or do next. When Julie spoke, Philip jumped.

'Shall I get us all some more coffee Philip, and something to eat maybe, what do you think?'

'Coffee, yes, thanks,' said Philip flatly.

'What do you think we should do?' ventured Darren.

'I think we should call the police,' offered Julie as she left to get the coffee.

'We could, but I doubt they would take very seriously a person not turning up for a party, even if we are sure it isn't as simple as that.'

'Philip, has Andi spoken to you about the paintings?' began Darren.

'Yes, she has, of course, you don't think . . .' whispered Philip.

'Well no, not really, it's just that . . .'

'What? Look, if you know something, you must tell me.'

'I guess I'm just thinking out loud. The business with the paintings was worrying Andi and I wondered if she had started asking awkward questions and got herself in trouble with the people at the sale-rooms.'

'It makes you wonder doesn't it? Had she said anything to you about taking her suspicions further?'

'Just sort of speculating about it you know, I think she would have talked to us about it before doing anything rash.'

'What, like talking to the police for instance?'

'Well, yes.'

There was an uncomfortable silence in which Philip and Darren followed their own lines of thought. Philip didn't want to elaborate about the paintings and hoped Julie and Maureen wouldn't ask. He was desperately worried about Andi, but he was reluctant to involve the police as that would mean telling them about the paintings. He was afraid Andi would be accused of forgery – a very serious offence. He could not tell his colleagues either.

'Do you think we *should* talk to the police?' asked Darren at last. He too was very worried. All he cared about was Andi's safety. He had not considered the possibility of a forgery charge.

'Not just yet, we must see if we can find Andi first. If she's OK, and I'm sure she must be, there's got to be a simple solution to this, hasn't there? Then we forget it. If not, for God's sake, Darren – what if not?'

'Then the police will have to know about her suspicions,' said Darren.

Philip had frightened himself with the possibilities and he had gone very pale, causing Julie and Maureen to fuss round him again.

By the time the last stragglers had gone home, leaving just Julie and Maureen, who had insisted on staying with Philip and Darren, it was almost three in the morning. They had explored every possibility regarding Andi's apparent disappearance and got nowhere.

'Look boys,' began Julie, 'why don't we try to get some sleep, then in the morning you can go to Andi's place. Chances are she'll have got back from wherever she's gone by then and we'll be able to laugh at ourselves for worrying unnecessarily. What do you think?'

'I'm sure you're right,' admitted Philip, and Darren nodded his agreement. They were so tired there was nothing they could have done even if they had received news of Andi. Philip's house had plenty of rooms and beds were made up, so it was a simple matter for them to get themselves to bed.

Philip slept on and off, dreaming of disasters. When he went downstairs at seven-thirty feeling more ragged than before, he found the other three sitting at the breakfast bar drinking black coffee in silence.

'What?' he asked, thinking they may have heard something.

'What?' replied Darren looking up from his cup. 'What do you mean?'

'Any news?'

'No, nothing at all. I've tried phoning Andi again, no reply. She's got one of those old-fashioned answerphone machines and it can't take any more messages. Who else is trying to find her do you think?'

'That's strange isn't it, we've left a few messages ourselves but not enough to fill up the system. So, what do we do? And why hasn't she phoned us. Surely if she was OK she would have phoned. Something has happened to her.

'All the more reason to tell the police,' insisted Darren.

'Anyone fancy some breakfast?' enquired Julie, 'we should eat something you know.'

'I don't fancy anything, but I suppose we should try to eat. What about some toast? Shall I do it?' offered Philip, anxious to avoid Darren's insistence on calling the police.

'No, I'll do it, have you got any bread?' Maureen was already on homing in on the toaster. Julie followed her. The two women busied themselves making toast and more coffee.

Philip and Darren decided they would go to Andi's house and if she wasn't there, ask some of her neighbours if they had seen her. Julie in the meantime would try phoning hospitals. The two men said they couldn't face doing that. The mood was bleak.

Darren looked up as he munched mechanically on a piece of toast, 'I don't know why we are looking at this so pessimistically you know, all we know is that Andi didn't turn up to a party that we know she was not keen on in the first place, and because she isn't at home. I mean – she could have gone to see some friends or something.' Darren was not addressing anyone in particular, and no-one answered. 'Well, that's right isn't it?' he persisted.

'Yes, maybe you are right,' conceded Philip, 'but she would have phoned, that's why I feel sure something is wrong. And last night you felt the same way. But whatever the reason, she would have phoned, surely.'

'Yes, I know, I'm just trying to convince myself we're being silly.'

Philip turned to Julie and Maureen. 'Do you mind staying on here for the time being, then if we hear anything we can let you know, and vice-versa of course.'

'That's fine with me,' said Julie, 'I'll check with the office that everything is OK there.'

'That would be good, thank you.'

'Come on then, let's get on with it. Whose car are we going in?' said Darren stuffing a last piece of toast into his mouth.

'What are you driving?'

'I've got an Astra. Why?'

'We'll go in yours then, mine will stick out too much in Andi's neighbourhood,'

'Does that matter?'

'It might if the painting guys are about. I don't want them to know we're on to them.'

'Are we on to them?'

'Well we know what they're up to don't we?'

'You're probably right, OK.'

'Thanks a lot Julie, you've been marvellous,' said Philip giving her a quick one-handed hug as he struggled into his coat. 'And you, Maureen, thanks very much for your help.'

'Take care!' shouted Julie as they went through the heavy front door.

6

Darren kept a key to Andi's flat because they often worked together. It had become his habit to just let himself in whenever he called. Philip thought it sounded a very strange relationship.

The flat, on the top floor of a converted warehouse, was deserted. Andi's new party dress lay limp and forlorn on the bed, there was no sign that she or anyone else had been in the flat since she laid it out. They looked round for anything that might give them a clue as to her whereabouts. They were just about to leave and begin asking neighbours if they had any news of Andi, when Darren stopped.

'The phone!' he exclaimed.

'I didn't hear it,' said Philip, almost out of the door.

'No, the messages, we can listen to find out who else was phoning her and filling up the message system!'

'Of course! I hadn't thought of that. Where is it?'

Most of the messages were from friends saying hello. One was from an artists' suppliers, and several were from themselves. It was looking very unlikely that there would be anything of any use when a message from earlier in the week began to play, causing the two men to listen more carefully.

'I've warned you, young lady. Stop being difficult. If you don't finish the painting by the end of the month and deliver it in the usual way, you will be in serious trouble. Phone me.'

'Do you recognise the voice?' asked Philip.

'No, I've never met the guys she paints for. She always goes to meet them on her own. It sounds ominous, don't you think?'

'It does, very. What was she working on? Do you know if she finished the painting?'

'No, she didn't mention it at all. She always seems to be working on something.'

'We could have a look in the studio, see if there is anything on her easel.'

They had only glanced in the studio just to check Andi was not there. Now they looked more closely, but not knowing what they were looking for.

Andi's studio was tiny but in every other way typical of an artist's studio, it even had a large angled skylight. Finished and unfinished canvasses, some framed, some unframed, were stacked against almost every wall, a bench covered with a clutter of jars of brushes and paint covered rags, pictures cut from magazines were pinned to a cork-board.

In the centre of the room stood an easel with a large photograph of a painting of a riverside scene with several people sitting on the grass. Darren leaned close to study it.

'She specialises in the impressionists as you know, that's a Manet. You can't mistake his work. She told me she had been asked to copy a Manet but said she couldn't do it,' said Darren. 'But it does rather look as if she might have started before going to stay with you.'

'It looks that way, but where is the painting?'

'Do you think that could be the painting the guy on the phone was referring to?'

'Looks like it. What else is there?' Darren scanned the room and looked at several canvasses that were stacked up against the wall. 'Most of these are Andi's own, but here's one of her Cassons. Have you seen them, they're very good,' said Darren, proudly holding up the painting for Philip to see. 'It's a pity she has to paint fakes instead of her own stuff. Of course she always says they are not forgeries, but copies for the owners to hang while the originals are stored safely. That's what she says anyway, and I daresay that is what she believes, but there is money in forgeries,' smiled Darren.

'So, what is the next step?'

'Talk to the neighbours. It's a very friendly area this, everybody knows everybody else's business and comings and goings.'

'Right, you lead the way then, as you know them,' said Philip, giving Darren a little push towards the door.

They spoke to Andi's immediate neighbours first but, although they were all keen to help, no-one had any news of Andi since about mid-day the day before. They asked the owner of the little corner shop and his customers.

'She came in for her bottle of milk as usual yesterday morning. I haven't seen her since. She often pops in two or three times throughout the day but not since the morning, as I say.'

'I saw her at about ten o'clock, she was heading towards the high street,' offered an elderly lady with a shopping trolley.

'Did you speak to her?' asked Darren.

'No, but she waved to me,' said the woman.

'Did she seem all right to you?'

'I think so, she smiled at me.'

The next stop was the off-licence, where Andi bought an occasional bottle of wine.

'She came in here at, ooh, elevenish I would say,' said the girl behind the counter. 'Bought a bottle of Australian red. Four pounds fifty it was. It's quite a nice one, we're selling a lot of it at the moment,' she added brightly.

'OK, thanks, you've been very helpful,' said Philip, as he turned to the door.

'Why was she buying wine? Surely not to bring to your party.' Darren mused, as they made their way back to Andi's flat.

'No, I wouldn't have thought so.'

'That message on the phone. He said deliver the painting as usual.'

'I've seen her deliver paintings; do you think she delivered this one?'

'Well if she did, why isn't she here. No, I think she didn't deliver the painting and they've taken her somewhere to force her to finish it. So, if that's the case, we really should tell the police, report a missing person.'

'No, not yet anyway,' said Philip. 'We don't want to risk her being associated with the forgery if we can help it, and although she will obviously be very distressed, they won't harm her, she's too useful to them,'

'Unless she had threatened to blow the whistle on their little scam and they panicked.'

'We need to find the guy she used to deliver the paintings to. He will know where she is being kept.'

'So, how do we find him?' asked Darren, not following Philip's train of thought.

'I have a drawing Andi did of the guy, so we'll know him if we see him. Where would they dispose of dodgy pictures? What about the galleries?'

'Oh, I see what you mean. The guy is going to be where the paintings are being sold. But I don't think any decent gallery would risk anything that was not kosher,' Darren said, 'It just isn't worth their while. No, it's likely to be auction houses in more out of the way places, or even abroad.' Darren suggested, 'or even private sales, to collectors.'

'Do you know the auctions houses yourself?'

'I know where they are. I've delivered stuff from time to time.'

'That's our next line of enquiry then, do you agree?'

'Yes, I can find out when there are going to be sales quite easily. But it's going to be a long old job going around all the sale-rooms.'

'I guess you're right. But we might as well make a start.'

'Not my scene, Phil. Thing is we're talking big money sales, aren't we? I mean, it wouldn't be worth their while if they were only going to sell a picture for a hundred quid would it?'

'No, but as you said, Sotheby's and outfits like that wouldn't risk selling anything dodgy, would they?'

'No, they wouldn't, but they're selling 'em somewhere. How do we find out? Let's just hope they aren't going abroad!'

'No, or private sales! We could try Christie's and Sotheby's and some of the other big firms first, if only to cross them off the list. We'll ask them when they've got sales on, and then go on from there if the paintings don't show up,' suggested Philip. 'This could take ages. We can't afford to delay. We've got to find Andi,' he said, banging the table so hard it made a pot of brushes jump and almost spill.

'Trouble is we've nothing else to go on, have we? We've got to start somewhere.'

They bought a paper from a newsagent's shop in Andi's street and studied the advertisements.

After a few minutes they had established that there was to be a sale at a small auction house not far from Andi's flat, that very day.

'I should think if they were trying to unload moderately priced dodgy paintings, one of the smaller auctions would be best, where it was unlikely they would be fussy about provenance and stuff like that,' ventured Darren. 'But they wouldn't be able to sell a painting as valuable as that Manet in a small sale.'

'Well we know, or we think we know that she hasn't finished the painting yet, so it wouldn't be that anyway.'

'No, that's right.'

'Andi said she didn't think they would sell the paintings in London, she thought the Midlands would be the best bet, but I suppose, we might as well start in London, as we're here.'

7

Andi laid out her new dress on the bed, ready to get into when she had showered and done her hair. This would be a new departure for her as she had never been to a party that involved dressing up like this, in fact she had never dressed up in such finery. She was excited at the prospect but still apprehensive about meeting lots of people she didn't know. Not that she wouldn't be suitably dressed, she felt sure the beautiful outfit Philip had paid for was as good as anything she would see on the other women at the party – it was just that she wasn't used to mixing in the sort of circles that Philip was used to. But, she was looking forward to it nevertheless and was about to go into the bathroom when the doorbell rang.

'Oh, who could that be?' she exclaimed, 'What a time to call'.

She was surprised to see one of the men for whom she was doing the paintings, standing there at her door.

'Oh, hello, Harry, what do you want? I'm getting ready to go out.'

'Sorry, love, the boss wants to see you.'

'Well, he can't, not now. I told you I'm getting ready to go out.'

'He wants to see you urgently. Get your coat, now.' Harry said sharply.

'No, I won't. I'll see him tomorrow.' Andi backed into the hallway and tried to close the door, but Harry had his foot in the way and pushed his way inside.

'I've tried to be nice, Miss, but if you won't cooperate I shall have to be rough. Now get your coat, it's cold.'

Andi could see that she had no choice, she could not fight off this man and he clearly could not be persuaded. She picked up her coat and handbag and allowed herself to be steered from the flat, down the stairs and into the waiting car.

'I've told Mr Beaumont that I'll finish the painting as soon as I can. You can't rush these things you know . . .' began Andi when they were in the car.

'You can tell Mr Beaumont that when you see 'im, Miss. It's no use talking to me,'

The driver had said nothing and seemed intent on getting away as quickly as possible. The traffic was not too heavy in the post rush hour period but there was still enough to hinder them, causing the driver to curse under his breath every time he came up behind a car he thought should be going faster.

When they had been going for more than half an hour Andi looked out of the window at unfamiliar streets and asked, 'Where are we going? I thought Mr Beaumont lived in Wood Green.'

'We aren't going to Mr Beaumont's house, Miss. Just be quiet. You'll see in good time.'

Andi became more and more anxious as they motored on into unknown territory. The rows of shops, so familiar in the London suburbs where Andi had grown up, were left behind to be replaced with rows of houses, and then even the houses were left behind, and the roads were lined with bushes and trees. Andi sat with her nose to the window, wondering where she was being taken. Out of the city there were few street lights and she couldn't see anything more than fleeting images of buildings and now and again a car. They were now far from London and she had no idea where they were.

The warmth and movement of the car made Andi sleepy and she slept uneasily.

It was still dark by the time the car slowed to turn into a tree-lined drive. Andi didn't know how long she had slept. The car stopped in front of a large house. Harry opened the door and took Andi's hand, not in a gentlemanly way, but to make sure she did not try to run away. They walked up a short path lined with bushes and entered the house by a side door.

'Where are we? Why have you brought me here?'

'Never mind that, just stay here,' said Harry sharply.

A few minutes later, Mr Beaumont, the only other person Andi had had any dealings with hitherto, came down the stairs and bade her follow him.

'Now, young lady,' he began, turning to face her as she followed him into a large sitting room. 'I've been very patient with you up to now, but you have let me down. You promised the painting by the end of last week and I need it urgently. So now I have to make sure you work on it, under supervision. I have all the facilities here. You'll work here until it is finished. Do you understand?'

'Well, I told you before, I was working on the painting, but it is not like the others – it can't be rushed – there are brushstrokes in thick paint that have to be just like the original, it's painstaking work. I was doing my best but . . .'

'I've had the painting brought here, and all your paints and stuff. You'll be fed, and you'll have your own room while you are here. I can't do any more. It is now up to you.'

'Harry, take the young lady upstairs.' He turned away and Harry once again took Andi's arm and began to lead her away.

'I can manage quite well myself thank you,' she said, shaking free of his grasp.

Upstairs, Andi found herself in a large open-plan area, rather like a large bed-sitting room. At one end was a bed and several armchairs, a television set and a coffee table and in a corner a tiny kitchen area with a small fridge, a sink and a microwave oven. Cupboards above the minuscule work-top were just big enough to contain the makings of a cup of tea or coffee.

The main area of the room, lit by a very large window, was set up as a studio. Andi's own jars of brushes and her box of paints were laid out on a bench. A professional easel stood in the centre of the room with the painting she had been working on in place. This was the sort of work space that Andi could only dream of.

She was standing, taking it all in, when Mr Beaumont came up the stairs.

'Well? What do you think? You have everything you need. Your food will be brought to you and all you have to do is ask for anything else you need.'

'Oh, it is wonderful, of course, I would love a proper studio of my own. But, not like this, dragged from my flat, without any warning or explanation. I was getting ready to go out when your goon came and grabbed me. I can't work like this. I refuse.'

'Oh, refuse, do you. Well we'll see about that. You promised to paint for me, Miss, and paint you will. You are getting paid, what are you complaining about?'

'I'm complaining about being taken forcibly from my home, that's what. And I demand to be taken back. I haven't refused to do your paintings up to now, but I can't work any faster. I am not sure that I'll do any more. I know what you're doing is illegal and I don't want any part of it.'

'As I said, young lady, you will paint – or there will be trouble.'

'What sort of trouble? You can't force me to paint.' Andi's voice had begun to tremble.

'If the authorities were to find out that you have forged works of art you would be considered as guilty as me. I'm going to leave you now.' He turned and left the room closing the door behind him.

Andi went to the door to shout after him but found the door locked. She pulled at the handle and banged as hard as she could, but there was no response.

She looked around her; the room was comfortable and warm. Beaumont had promised to pay her and feed her if she painted the pictures, and if she didn't he would expose her as a forger. What choice did she have? But it was not Andi's nature to give in to threats and coercion. She banged on the door again, shouting to be let out.

After banging and shouting for several minutes and getting no reply, Andi walked to the end of the room and sat on the bed in the living area. She felt defeated. Even if she had wanted to, she couldn't have done any painting. The way she felt, any attempt would be useless. She looked out of the big picture window. All she could see was the dimly lit driveway to the house, lined with trees and bushes. The car she had been brought in was not on the drive. She craned her neck to see closer to the house but still could not see a car. She pulled a chair over to the window and stood on it. The additional height gave her a view of the drive almost immediately below the window. There was no sign of a car. Had they gone, leaving her to make up her mind?

Thinking of escape, Andi looked at the fastenings on the window. Several panes of the window could be opened outwards but not wide enough to get through, and even if she could get through, how would she reach the ground? That was no good, and in any case her captors more than likely had not left her on her own. Frustrated, she sat down again and tried to think how she could get away. Eventually she fell asleep.

8

When Andi woke, nothing had changed, there was no sound. It was beginning to get light outside, but the lights of the studio still burned brightly so the window looked quite dark. Andi's watch said half past eight, but was that in the morning or the evening, she could not think for a moment. Then recollection of recent events hit her. She had been brought here last night, she had slept all night and now it was morning. She was hungry and thirsty, and just as she was wondering about food, the door opened and a man she had not seen before came in, carrying a tray.

'Breakfast, Miss. If there's anything else you want, just ring the bell,' the man said pleasantly. He pointed to a button by the door as he left and closed the door behind him.

'Yes, there is, I need a toilet and a shower.'

'There's a toilet in the corner there, and a wash basin. You'll have to manage with that.'

Andi opened the door in the corner of the room that she hadn't noticed before. Inside was a toilet and a tiny wash basin and a rail with several towels. 'I can't wash in that!' she shouted. The man ignored her. He left the room and closed the door behind him.

Andi looked at the breakfast tray. There was a bowl of cereal, a jug of milk, a small glass of fruit juice, a cafetière and a cup and saucer.

'The prisoner ate a hearty breakfast,' Andi muttered. She picked up the glass of fruit juice and drank it, then pushed down the plunger of the cafetière. She did not feel hungry any more. She sat down on the bed again and drank some coffee. It was bitter; they had not given her any sugar.

'How can I possibly be expected to work like this?' she said to herself. She lay down on the bed, curled up and wept.

Some time later, the man came back for the tray.

'You haven't eaten your breakfast,' he said. 'Would you like something different?'

'I can't eat. I want to go home,' wailed Andi, breaking down in tears.

'Oh dear, I'm sorry, you can't do that, love.'

Andi was surprised at the man's evident sympathy.

'Couldn't you help me to get away?'

'No, sorry, love, I am paid to keep you here and look after you.'

'Do you know why I'm being held here?' Andi asked.

'Doing some painting for Mr Beaumont, I understand.'

'Yes, that's right, against my will. I have been kidnapped. And you are an accessory. Whether you were aware or not of what was happening, you will be put in prison for kidnap, and it's a very long sentence. If you let me go, it will go in your favour.'

'I would probably be dead before anyone found out about you being kidnapped. I'm sorry, really, but there's nothing I can do.'

'You seem a decent chap, how did you get mixed up in this?' Andi asked, desperately trying to win the man over.

'I was just an ordinary burglar, never did nobody any harm, then I was asked to help out on a job. It seemed OK and the pay was good, so I did it, but then there was more jobs and they got a bit more, what you might call dodgy. But I couldn't pull out by then. They aren't nice people, Miss, believe me.'

'Oh, I believe you. What's your name?'

'I won't tell you my name in case you tell the cops. You can call me Bernie, Bernard is my second name. OK?'

'Right oh, Bernie. Thank you. It seems you are in as much of a jam as me.'

'If that's all, Miss . . .'

'Yes, I think so. Oh, where can I get a shower?'

'You'll have to manage with the little washbasin in the toilet, I'm afraid. I can't let you out of this room.' With that, and a wry smile, Bernie left and closed the door.

Regretting refusing to eat breakfast, Andi sat down again and considered her options. The sooner she finished the painting, the sooner they would let her go. Wouldn't they? But then it struck her that she knew too much about the kidnappers. A chill struck her. No, they could not let her go. What would they do with her? She was useful to them, so they would want to keep her locked up, painting forgeries. She could not work like that, could she? But she would have to if there was no alternative.

Philip would come looking for her, of course. But he could have no idea what had happened to her. Nobody knew what had happened to her. She didn't know herself where she was.

She got up and began to pace up and down the room, trying desperately to think.

She stopped in the middle of the room and looked at the canvas she had begun. A copy, no, she reminded herself, a forgery, of a Manet. She had made a start before going to stay with Philip. She smiled, she liked Manet's paintings. She had repaired several and enjoyed working on them.

Perhaps if she made an effort she would get lost in the work and maybe feel better about her plight. There was nothing else she could do, and if she did nothing she would go out of her mind with boredom.

Studying the rough outlines she had made, she began to think about the next step, then she stopped. Where was the photograph? The near full size, high resolution photograph of the original painting, from which she was working. She looked around the studio. There was no sign of it. She could not work without it. She might be able to produce a pastiche of a Manet – something in his style, but not a copy, a copy that would fool most collectors.

She pressed the bell push. Bernie came almost at once.

'Yes, Miss. What is it?' he said, standing in the doorway.

'I don't have the photograph. I can't work without it.'

'What photograph is that, Miss?'

'There is a large photograph of a painting in my studio at home. I need it to work on the copy.'

'Oh, I see. I'll tell Mr Beaumont.'

'Is he here?' asked Andi, surprised.

'No, he's gone back to London. I'll phone him.'

'Who else is here?'

'Only Reg. Just me and Reg, that's all. Reg is a cook. He will be getting your meals.' Bernie smiled. 'OK, Miss, I'd better phone Mr Beaumont.'

9

The auction house was an old chapel not far from Andi's flat. Philip and Darren had got there in plenty of time so that they could look at the paintings on sale.

They were surprised to see rows of assorted chairs haphazardly arranged amongst pieces of furniture and large sculptures. The walls were lined with paintings and photographs. At the front, at what had been the chapel's communion table, sat the auctioneer, consulting his watch. There were very few people in the room. The auctioneer looked at his watch every few seconds.

'Do you think you would be able to recognise one of Andi's paintings, Darren? I mean if they are so good, surely only a real expert would know they were phoney,' said Philip, as he scanned the catalogue.

'I couldn't tell you if a painting was genuine or not, but I might recognise a painting that Andi has been working on in the studio. I'm just hoping the guy we have the drawing of turns up.'

'Look, at this stage it's the guy we need. If he turns up, we can get him to tell us where Andy is being held.'

'How are we going to make him tell us?' asked Philip.

'I don't know, we'll grab him and give him a bit of a doing over.'

'I suppose,' mumbled Philip, thinking Darren was an unlikely person to 'do anyone over.''

'And if he is trying to sell a dodgy painting, we can tell the auctioneer.'

The sale-room was filling up slowly, the auctioneer was still looking at his watch.

The two men took seats near the door, so they could watch people coming in. Darren thought he might just recognise somebody, and Philip would watch for the man he'd seen Andi pass the paintings to. He looked again at Andi's drawing of the man.

More people had come into the saleroom and having consulted his watch one more time, the sale got under way. Philip was surprised how quickly the paintings sold. He looked round at people who were bidding large sums for paintings he would not have given house room to. 'This is all very new to me, Darren,' he whispered.

'Oh, me too. Interesting though.'

'Lot one hundred and fourteen, a fine oil on canvas by A.J.Casson,' intoned the auctioneer.

'Could that be one of Andi's?' whispered Philip, 'you said she had done Cassons.'

'It could be, I suppose, but I couldn't be sure. Listen.'

'Who will start me at thirty thousand pounds – Twenty then – twenty I have, twenty-five, thirty, thirty-five, any more? I'm selling at thirty-five thousand . . . thirty-seven five hundred, new bidder. Forty thousand, thank you sir, forty thousand pounds, I'm selling at forty thousand pounds, last chance . . . ' He tapped his gavel, 'Sold.'

The sales went on in similar fashion, some selling for hundreds, some thousands, but there had been no more paintings that might have been painted by Andi; at least none that Darren thought he had seen before. Neither had they seen the man that might lead them to Andi.

'This is hopeless, Darren. We'll never find anything this way. I vote we go.'

'Yeah, you're right. OK, so what do you suggest?'

'I just don't know, Darren. Keep trying I suppose. We've nothing else to go on. We just have to find the guy I've seen Andi with.'

'OK, so we find the next sale.

'That's about it, yes,' Philip agreed.

Philip had decided to stay in London rather than keep going back to Peterborough, or to his father's house in Letchworth. He had booked in to a small hotel not far from Andi's flat in Camden. It was pretty basic, but Philip was not interested in home comforts.

Over the course the next few weeks Philip and Darren became regular attenders at most of the smaller auctions in London. They had been surprised how many there were, and how many people attended, and even more surprised at the amount of money that was changing hands. They had learned a lot, but still had not seen the man who might lead them to Andi. Nor could they be sure that any of Andi's paintings had been sold.

They had arranged to meet at an auction house in West Norwood, south of the river, and because his car was in Peterborough Philip was having to use the underground. He was getting quite adept at navigating the system and it had only taken him about forty-five minutes to get from his hotel to the saleroom, including a change at Balham.

The two men sat in silence while a variety of prints and drawings were put up and dealt with very rapidly.

A number of paintings by artists Philip had never heard of, sold for prices ranging from a few hundred pounds to several thousand pounds. Each time a painting was held up Philip looked at Darren, who shook his head.

An attractive oil by Francis Nicholson, a view of London from the river, had an estimate of one to two thousand pounds, and after a rapid exchange sold for fifteen hundred pounds.

'I wouldn't have minded that one myself,' said Philip. But it was not one of Andi's, Darren was sure.

Another oil, of a horse, estimated at three to four thousand, didn't sell. And so it went on, painting after painting, some for just a hundred or so, and one for only twenty pounds.

A very small painting by John Constable made Philip sit up and take notice. Estimated at between twenty and thirty thousand pounds, it sold for three hundred and five thousand pounds.

'Wow!' said Philip, 'did you see that. It would be worth while copying one like that.'

'Yes, but the well-known artists like him would have bags of provenance. Andi wouldn't do those.'

'The Manet would have even more provenance than that, surely, and we think she's doing one of his.'

'That's true. Listen.' Darren was looking at the painting being held up. 'That's nice.'

'Nice oil by William Shayer, shore scene with horse and harbour,' intoned the auctioneer. 'Who will give me a thousand pounds? A thousand, thank you sir. Now this is a fine piece ladies and gentlemen, bound to go up in value, would look lovely over your fireplace. Fifteen hundred pounds, who will give two thousand? Seventeen fifty, thank you sir, any more now. No, sorry then, that one is not sold.'

'Didn't reach it's reserve,' said Darren. Too big I suppose. Nice picture though.'

'Yes, it would have looked good in my house,' said Philip.

'Why didn't you bid for it then?' asked Darren.

'I couldn't afford to spend that sort of money on a painting. I'll get Andi to do some for the house.'

'None of hers here, I'm afraid,' said Darren.

'No, and no sign of our man either. Come on, let's go.'

They drove back to Andi's flat in Darren's Astra, as it was a convenient central place to meet, and discussed their situation.

'We're no further on, are we?' said Darren, as he made coffee in Andi's tiny kitchen.

'No, we're not. I don't know what to suggest. We've been to lots of auctions and not seen the guy that Andi used to take work to. We haven't seen any of Andi's paintings . . .'

'Or we don't think we have,' corrected Darren.

'No, that's right. But even if we did see one that might be hers, without the man to make the connection, we would be none the wiser.'

'I'm going to have to go back to Peterborough to see how things are going in the office, do you want to stay here?'

'Might as well, there's nothing else I can do,' said Darren, passing a mug to Philip. 'No sugar, I'm afraid. Andi's run out.'

'She must be desperate, poor girl, all by herself, locked up, thinking we have abandoned her.'

'I know, I can't bear to think of it.'

'Any ideas,' said Philip, when he'd finished his coffee.

'No, you get off, I'll be in touch if anything turns up.'

'I guess we shall have to start in the Midlands, have a look, see what's coming up.'

'Yes, will do, I'll let you know. Keep in touch anyway, yes?'

'Yes, will do. Bye, take care.'

Once more, Philip wished he had his car, and settled down to another dreary train journey.

'Any news?' asked Julie when he got back to the office.

'No, nothing, I'm afraid. How are things here? Are you coping?'

'Yes, don't you worry, everything is fine,' Julie assured him.

Everything was ticking over nicely in the office in his absence, and he thought to himself, he'd better be careful, or they might think they could do without him permanently.

*

Andi, meanwhile, two weeks into her incarceration, was making the most of her situation by getting on with the painting. While very angry about being made to do the work, she had decided the best way to pass the time and to give her the best chance of getting away was to do what was required of her.

She loved painting and when she was working she thought of nothing else but the accuracy of her brushstrokes and perfectly matching colours.

Mr Beaumont had looked in a couple of times to check on progress and insisting that time was running out. He had not commented on the painting and Andi had concluded that he didn't know much about art.

10

Having made sure everything was running smoothly, Philip once more returned to the capital to meet up with his new friend and ally at Andi's flat, which Darren had adopted as his base.

Darren, with typical emotion, said how pleased he was to see Philip, but managed not to give him a hug.

'There's a sale in Nottingham on Wednesday, we could try that. What do you think?'

'Yes, OK, it's as good as anywhere. Do you know Nottingham?'

'Been there a couple of times. Went to a ballet at the Theatre Royal, and I've been to the Arts Theatre, too. There are several galleries and a good college of art. It's quite an arty town, so it might be a good place to start.'

'OK, we could give it a try, I remember Andi saying dodgy paintings might get through in the sticks. But isn't there one closer to home before that?'

'There's one in South Ken on Monday. We might as well go to that as it's near. Starts at ten thirty.'

'What are we going to do until then?' asked Philip.

'I've been having another look at Andi's paintings. I think we should familiarise ourselves with her style, so that if we see one, we'll know it's hers.'

'I don't think that's much good. I thought you were familiar with her paintings,' and her, a bit too familiar for my liking, Philip thought, 'But if they're copies, they won't look like her work, will they? Her own stuff, good as it is, won't fetch the sort of money these crooks are interested in. I mean, they could sell all her paintings if they wanted to. Who's to stop them?'

'How do you mean?' asked Darren.

'We know they can get into her flat, they already have, and they didn't take her paintings.'

'No, they didn't did they,' agreed Darren, thoughtfully.

'No, what we have to do is keep watching out for the guy she takes the paintings to. He's our only link, and the only one who might know where she is being held.'

'Yes, and I suppose he could be at any sale, even if Andi's pictures were not on sale.'

'Exactly.'

'So, have we been wasting our time looking for Andi's paintings?'

'No, not at all, because if her paintings were on sale, the guy that picked them up from her is likely to be there as well, to pick up his money. Don't you see?'

'Ye–es,' said Darren uncertainly. 'Right. And if we do see the guy, what then?'

'Good question. Do we tackle him, follow him – or what?'

'I don't know, take a photograph and tell the police?'

'Yes, I suppose, do you think they'll do anything?'

They debated their options for a while but gave up without coming to any conclusions.

'Come on, let's go and eat, then have an early night. We need to be fresh in the morning,' Darren suggested.

'Good idea, are you sleeping here now?' Philip asked.

'No, my place is only around the corner. I look in as often as I can. Are you still OK with your grotty hotel?' He laughed.

The auction house, not far from the Victoria and Albert Museum, was well attended, there were few seats left so the two men stood at the back among assorted pieces of brown furniture that looked as if they had been there for decades. Pictures of varying quality lined the walls among pieces of sculpture and hundreds of pots of all shapes and sizes.

The items to be sold were gathered at the front. An assistant was holding up a painting.

'Look, Darren, keep your eyes peeled, OK,' advised Philip.

Several paintings were sold in quick succession. None of the them looked familiar.

A few good quality paintings took longer to sell and went for quite high prices. None of them looked anything like the paintings Andi produced.

'This is a waste of time, Philip, don't you think?' whispered Darren.

Then just as Philip was trying to think how to respond, he spotted a familiar face.

'See that man that's just come in, navy blue suit, regimental tie? Don't let him see you looking. I don't want him to see me. I know him. I'm going to get behind that pillar where he won't see me.'

'Is he the guy?' asked Darren, all agog.

'No, but he might be just as important. Wait here.'

The newcomer took a seat close to the auctioneer's rostrum and opened a catalogue.

Darren crossed the room and stood beside Philip. Leaning against the pillar as nonchalantly as he could he asked, 'Who is he then?'

'Can't tell you now, just watch – see what he does.'

'Lot one hundred and thirty, a fine oil painting by Francis Picabia entitled *Au bord de la mer*. Shall we say one hundred thousand pounds? Eighty then. Eighty I have. Ninety thousand, and a half, this is a beautiful painting and worth much more – one hundred thousand, thank you sir, and one – one hundred and one thousand pounds. One hundred and two thousand, new bidder. One oh two, one oh three, one oh four, now we're getting there . . .' The auctioneer was well into his stride as the bidding went up to a hundred and fifty thousand pounds.

'Hundred and fifty, wow!' said Darren in a loud whisper.

'Sh, listen,' commanded Philip.

The price went up and up with several people taking bids on the telephone until the painting sold for two hundred thousand pounds. Philip could not be sure who had been the successful bidder.

There was some activity at the front of the room and Philip was craning his neck to see. The man in the blue suit was shaking hands with a tall, casually dressed young blond man.

'Bloody hell, Phil, did you see that? Two hundred thousand for a Francis Picabia. I've seen several of his paintings, I like them actually, but wow!'

'Wasn't there one of his in Andi's studio? Or at least a copy of a painting in a very similar style?'

'I do believe you're right. I think there was. Not that one, we only saw the one in her studio yesterday, but it could be one of hers. Wow!'

Anxious to get out of the saleroom without being seen by the man he recognised, Philip urged Darren towards the exit.

'Let's get well away and I'll tell you who that was,' he said, as they crossed the road and walked towards South Kensington Underground Station.

'Why don't we take a taxi?' asked Darren as they were about to enter the station.

'Wait a minute, I've got an idea,' said Philip, holding Darren's arm. 'If we could get into the back room of the auction somehow, have a closer look at the paintings – we could perhaps see if any of them were Andi's, and especially that Picabia. What do you think?'

'Well, as I said, I might recognise some I suppose, if I've seen them in her studio, or if she had been working on them. But how are we going to get in?'

'How about if you put on a brown warehouse coat and carry a clip-board. Or better still, carry a painting. You could just walk in, nobody would take any notice of you.'

'You are volunteering me for this job, are you?' said Darren, doubtful of the idea now.

'It's no use me going, I don't know the paintings.'

'No, of course. OK, I'll do it. Where do we get a warehouse coat from?'

'That should be easy enough, I'm sure there will be one in my old office. It's not very far from here. We get the coat, pick up one of Andi's paintings and in you go!' Philip seemed very pleased with his idea. Darren was not so keen.

'What if I am challenged?'

'Just say you're from Burford's.'

'Why Burford's?'

'I don't know, It's as good a name as any. They won't check. It'll be OK, you'll see.'

'Andi's is nearest, we'll pick up a canvas then go to my firm's head office and grab a coat. Then come back here. It won't take more than half an hour.'

Taking a taxi as Darren had suggested, they were soon back at Andi's flat and Darren picked a canvas from the stack against the wall in the studio. The taxi then took them to Baker Street and while the taxi weaved through the traffic on the short journey, Philip told Darren who the mystery man was.

'His name is Sedgewick, he works in my office. I'd love to know what he is doing buying expensive paintings.'

'Well, if he's got a top job he can probably afford to buy expensive paintings,' suggested Darren.

'It's not that top a job, I assure you. He couldn't afford to buy paintings worth that much.'

'Yes, but perhaps he wasn't buying. He could have been selling.'

'Whatever he was doing, he's one of them, I'm sure of it,' said Philip.

'You can't be sure of that, just on what you've seen.'

'No, maybe not but I have strong feeling I'm right.'

11

As Philip had predicted, it was a simple matter to borrow a brown warehouse coat from Andy, the caretaker of the insurance company. The offer of a handsome tip had ensured the taxi waited the few minutes it took, and they were back at the auction house in little more than forty minutes.

'Right, in you go,' said Philip, gently pushing Darren in the direction of the door to the side of the rostrum where they had seen people taking lots.

Darren, with canvas under his arm strode confidently through the door into the store-room at the rear of the auction house.

Philip waited, willing his new friend success.

After what to Philip had seemed an awfully long time, Darren emerged from the back room, still carrying Andi's painting. He walked as calmly as he could until he was outside.

'How did you get on?' asked Philip. 'Did you see any of Andi's work?'

'I told you it would be difficult. There are hundreds of paintings in there, all on racks, waiting to be sold, I suppose, and some already sold waiting for collection or delivery to their new owners.'

'Yes, yes, of course, but did you see any of Andi's?' pressed Philip.

'I honestly couldn't swear to it, but, yes, I think there may have been some of Andi's. I'm sorry, Philip, I couldn't be sure.'

'Oh, OK, well, it was worth a try, I think we are on the right track. What do we do now?'

'You tell me.'

'Back to Andi's'

'I can't see what we'll gain from going through Andi's paintings again Phil. We know she did a painting that looked very much like a Casson. Even if I had seen one in the store room, what would it have proved?'

'It wouldn't prove anything. It would just confirm that she is doing forgeries of paintings that are likely to come up on the market as genuine.'

'As against what?'

'Rather than just copies of paintings that collectors want to be able to show while their valuable paintings are in the bank.'

'But they could be sold, surely. The collectors could sell the real painting and keep a copy for their own enjoyment.'

'Mm. I suppose. I would still like to see if she has signed the paintings.'

'Fair enough. I just can't see how that is going to help us find her,' argued Darren, later, as he put his key in the lock.

'Let's be systematic about this, we'll start with the ones piled against the wall and move them one by one to the table. I'll photograph them with my phone as we go,' said Philip, pointing to the stacks of paintings they had looked at before.

Fifteen minutes later Philip had a record of all the paintings in the first pile and they began to examine the second stack.

'This looks like a Casson to me,' said Darren as he lifted a painting for Philip to photograph.

'It certainly has that look about it. Is there a signature?

'There is, look, clear as a bell. But if she is making fakes not just honest copies – should they be signed at all?'

'That, my friend, is a very good point. What about the others?'

'I don't know most of these painters,' said Darren, 'but one thing I can tell you; these are not Andi's signature. It looks very much to me as if she is doing fakes.' He stood looking at Philip with a stunned expression. 'Oh Andi, what have you got yourself into?'

'I'm afraid you're right. Come on let's get the rest of them photographed,' said Philip, checking that his phone was recording the images satisfactorily.

Taking one last look round the studio, they made ready to leave.

'You know, Phil, I'm sure Andi isn't deliberately making fakes. I think she is the innocent victim of a fraud. They have persuaded her that the paintings she is doing are simply as she told us, copies for the personal use of owners. They persuaded her to sign the pictures so that the owners could show their friends the paintings and claim them to be the originals.'

'Yes, that could well be it, of course. But the fact remains, even if she was being made to do it and not aware of the significance of what she was doing, she is still guilty of forgery. We've got to find her and get her out of this.'

'What do you suggest, Philip, talk to the police now?'

'Yes, I think we must now. But just report a missing person. Don't tell them about our suspicions about the paintings. Not just yet.'

As Philip had feared, the police did not seem very interested, although they were surprised that they had not reported Andi missing earlier. Hundreds of people go missing in London, some deliberately, and there is little they can do. It would be logged of course, and they would do what they could, but don't hold out too much hope.

'At least they have it logged now and if anything should come to light they'll know about it. Now, I'm sorry Darren, but I must get back to Peterborough. I have a business to run. I'll keep in touch on the phone and I'll come down to London again as soon as I can. Okay?'

'Yeah, yeah, of course,' said Darren distractedly. 'See you then.'

12

Philip went back north by train and took a taxi from the station to the office.

He was confident in his new staff and if anything had required his personal attention they would have got in touch, but he felt happier being at the coalface himself, checking that everything was in order.

'Good morning, Philip,' said Julie, brightly, as she brought Philip's first cup of coffee of the day from the little kitchen next door to the office. 'Is everything all right? Have you heard from Andi?'

'No, Julie, I haven't heard, and I am very worried. We've reported her missing, but I am going to talk to the police again and tell them the whole story.'

'I'll get them for you,' said Julie, leaving the office.
A moment later the phone dinged to indicate the call had been put through. Philip explained as succinctly as possible the events leading up to the disappearance of Andi and his suspicions about the art fraud. The police, not known for their alacrity when it comes to missing persons, sat up and took notice at the mention of fraud. They would start making enquiries immediately.

Julie came into the office again, with a pile of post, which she had opened and put into folders depending on the subject matter. Nothing appeared to be too pressing, so Philip picked up the company newsletter which was on top of the pile.

The headline on the front page congratulated one of the company's agents for landing a huge premium for insuring a painting which was due to be sent to the United States.

The article went on to say that a painting by Manet was to be lent to a gallery in Washington and the lender had insisted on the painting being insured for five million pounds. The premium on such a sum was understandably very high and would be paid by the gallery. The commission alone would run into hundreds of pounds.

Philip's blood had run cold at the sight of the article, and as he read it again he had visions of a web of intrigue and fraud beyond his comprehension.

He buzzed for Julie to come in to the office. She came in, smiling.

'You've seen the newsletter I expect? Do you know the name of the agent that arranged the insurance on the painting?'

'Sandra from motor said she thought it was Andrew Shaw. He's a broker in the City somewhere.'

'Thank you, you don't happen to know who he deals with in the office do you?'

'No, but I can ask. Give me a minute?'

'Yes, see what you can find out. Thanks, Julie.'

Julie left the office and Philip sat thinking of all the possible implications of insuring the painting. There may be no connection at all and the agent was in all probability completely innocent, but wouldn't it be an extraordinary coincidence, all things considered, if someone in his own company was mixed up in this art fraud business?

What were they doing with the paintings that Andi was producing? He needed to talk to someone about it but could think of no one he could trust sufficiently. He walked over to the window. It was raining, the cathedral was only just visible through the gloom, appearing to float above the rooftops of the old town. He thought of his and Andi's recent visit to the cathedral.

Julie knocked and entered, looking pleased with herself. Philip surreptitiously wiped a tear from his eye.

'Right, I thought Sandra would know – she has her nose to the ground,' she laughed briefly and continued. 'Sandra said Andrew Shaw brings in quite a lot of business. He always goes up to the third floor but she's not really sure who he deals with, although she had seen him talking to Sally, Mr Sedgewick's secretary. You know, the girl with the long red hair?'

Philip knew exactly who Sally was; he would be a very unusual man if he hadn't noticed the girl.

Stewart Sedgewick was one of the firm's high flyers; he was also the man Philip had seen at the auction house.

Philip was only on nodding terms with Sedgewick as he not had dealings with him at Head Office. Since he had transferred to Peterborough on the recommendation of the MD, after Philip's initial staffing round, he hadn't had a chance to talk to him. He wasn't even sure what part of the business he specialised in. He would speak to one of his old team who had opted to stay at Head Office. He might know about the business Sedgewick was doing.

'Hi, William, Philip – How are you?' he said when he was put through to William Fenton.

'Hello, Philip, gosh, good to hear from you. How's it going in the sticks? They tell me you actually like it up there.'

'Yes, I do as a matter of fact. You should reconsider. Get some fresh air into your lungs.'

'Not for me, I like a bit of carbon monoxide and diesel fumes.'

'Funny man, look, the reason I'm phoning – I just heard about that big premium Sedgewick has landed. What do you know about him?'

'Only what you already know, I guess. Maltby was very keen for him to go to Peterborough for some reason, I know that.'

'Can you put your ear to the ground and find out why he was transferred. I wasn't consulted, and it seems very strange.'

'I thought you must have been involved in his transfer. You know the old man wants to divide the company's business up between the branches. Eventually there will be more branches in the shires and each one will have a speciality – surely you know that?'

'No, I don't. It's all new to me, and I don't like the idea at all. Why hasn't Maltby spoken to me about it? Is it common knowledge down there?'

'I'm not sure about common knowledge. I just happened to overhear old Sowerbridge talking to someone in the loos. I was in a cubicle so I couldn't see who he was talking to. Nothing has been said officially.'

'Right, so it might just be an idea the old man is bandying about, you think?'

'Quite likely, I reckon.'

'Is the old man in the office today, do you know?' asked Philip.

'He is, yes, I nearly bumped into his Roller when we were both trying to park this morning. I thought he was going to kill me. He would have done if I'd scratched the thing.'

'He would too. You be careful! Thanks a lot for the info. And think about coming to Peterborough. You'd love it.'

'Sorry, not me. Good to talk, take care. Cheers.'

That piece of information had thoroughly thrown Philip, and while he was thinking of its implications his mobile phone rang.

'Darren! Any news?' he said, recognising the number, before Darren could speak.

'Well, not exactly, but I think I have a bit of a lead. Can you come down?'

'Yes, in fact I had this very minute decided to go to the London office. What have you got?'

'You know the photograph that was on her easel? Well, it's gone.'

'Gone? How do you mean?'

'I went to Andi's flat this morning just to see if she had come back – well, no, just to be there and feel near to her somehow I suppose, and I noticed the picture had gone.'

'When was the last time you saw it?'

'I don't know, it may have gone weeks ago, I just didn't notice.'

'Was there any sign of a break-in or anything?'

'Nothing, I've phoned the police. They didn't seem much interested.'

'They wouldn't. OK, Darren, I'm on my way. Where shall I see you?'

'Might as well come to Andi's flat I guess. How long will you be?'

'Not much more than an hour and a half, all being well.'

'OK then, bye.'

13

Traffic on the A1(M) was unusually heavy and by the time he had battled through the lunch-time traffic in the city it was past two o'clock when Philip eventually knocked on the door of Andi's flat.

'I thought you'd got lost, Phil,' said Darren as he opened the door. 'Come on in.'

'Now what's all this about a missing painting?'

'Not a painting, a photograph of a painting,'

'I don't understand. What are you saying? A photograph is missing?'

'Yes, a large photograph of a painting by Manet. I think Andi was copying it, and now it is gone.'

'There wasn't a painting on the easel was there?'

'No, don't you remember? The easel was empty when we came to the flat. They took the painting when they took Andi, but they didn't take the photograph that she was working from. They came back for it.'

'I see,' said Philip, not really seeing at all.

'I am as sure as I can be that that is what happened, Phil. And if she is copying stuff in the big league – I mean, Manets are fabulously expensive – well, she will be in big trouble if she gets caught.'

'How long would it take to do a Manet do you think Darren?'

'I've no idea, if I spent a year, I couldn't produce a Manet, but Andi might do one in a week or so I suppose, it would depend on whether she was using materials that Manet would have used or modern ones.'

'Why is that, what difference would it make?'

'Lots. The experts can analyse pigments and some modern colours were not available at the turn of the century, so a new colour would give the game away instantly. Modern paints dry a whole lot quicker and it could affect the way colours are blended on the canvas. The impressionists worked quite fast as a rule and the original might only have taken days to complete. But to copy such a painting, getting all the brushstrokes right, could take ages. Superficially, they could look exactly the same. Why do you ask?'

'My firm has just insured a painting that is being sent to America, on loan to a museum. It was a Manet.'

'Oh, do you think the painting Andi was working on could be the very one, and they have taken it to wherever they are keeping her, to finish? But wouldn't that be the most extraordinary coincidence?'

'How do you mean?'

'That they asked your firm to insure a painting that was done by your girlfriend – I mean, out of all the insurance companies – and why go to one in Peterborough when they are based in London?'

'I don't think they even know about me. The underwriter used to be in our London office, but has recently transferred to Peterborough. The agent who dealt with him in London would probably want to continue to deal with him wherever he went. It's good to deal with people you know. Of course, if they do know of my connection, that would give them more leverage.'

'Oh, yeah, I see what you mean. They think you will be obliged to take on the insurance because you know Andi?'

'I thought you were bright, Darren. Yes. That's it, ' said Philip, getting exasperated. 'Are Andi's paints still here?'

'Oh, I see what you mean. I didn't think of that. Let's see – there are some tubes and a few brushes on the table by the easel, but I didn't notice her big box of paints, and several jars of brushes are missing. You're right, they have taken them. We just didn't notice because it's much harder to see things that aren't there than things that are.'

Philip gave Darren an odd look, but of course he was right. 'I need to find out more about the painting we are insuring. I'll get the office to send the information down here by courier.'

While they waited for the information to arrive, there was nothing constructive Philip and Darren could do, so they decided to have something to eat. Darren knew an Italian restaurant quite near Andi's flat.

Although the food was good, neither man really enjoyed it. They could only think of Andi's predicament and their inadequate attempts to find her. Two hours later, they were back in Andi's flat, pacing up and down like a couple of expectant fathers.

'It's times like this I wish I still smoked,' said Darren. 'Do you fancy a cup of tea or coffee – I've got to do something.'

When the doorbell rang, Philip ran to the door and wrenched it open, startling the courier. He signed for the package and was tearing it open even before he closed the door. Inside were photographs of a painting, copies of the forms giving details of the painting, the dimensions of the painting itself and of its frame.

'Would you recognize the painting in the photograph, Darren?' Philip said, handing him the photograph.

'I couldn't swear to it, but it certainly looks like the one in the photograph. Yes, I think so,'

There was a receipt for two million dollars on the headed notepaper of a well-known auction house, and a hand-written appraisal of the painting saying that as far as the writer could ascertain it was a genuine Manet. It was signed but the signature was illegible. Another document, on the letter heading of a Bond Street art gallery, valued the painting at five million pounds for insurance purposes. A short typed note from a firm of solicitors in Gloucester stated that the insurance was required for the sum of five million pounds, payable in the event of loss, by theft, fire or any other means of destruction, to a Percival Trentham Fielding. The letter stated that the contact address for Mr Fielding was that of his solicitors.

'I don't think any of this is genuine, Darren,' said Philip after reading through all the papers several times. I'd have to check of course, but I'm a bit doubtful about the Bond Street gallery. Have you ever heard of Kleitner's?'

'Well no, but I don't move in those circles exactly.'

'I'm going to my office, Darren, to see what I can sort out with this. Are you going to be alright on your own? You can come with me if you like.'

'No. I'd better stay here in case. You go, but keep in touch. What's your office number if I need to phone you?'

Philip gave Darren his card, then took it back to write his mobile number on the back.

'There you are. If I'm not in the office, try the mobile, but if I'm in the car I may not be able to answer straight away. I'll get back as soon as I can.' He tried to give Darren a reassuring smile, but it didn't quite work, and Darren's face crumpled.

Philip ran down the stairs and out to his car. By now the traffic was in full spate and it was a long time before he could even get out of his parking space. Once on the road north again, traffic was moving quicker, and it wasn't long before he was on the A1(M) again on his way to Peterborough, driving as fast as the traffic allowed.

As soon as he arrived back in the office, he found out where Sedgewick's office was and barged in.

Sedgewick looked up, startled. 'Hello, Mr Harding, what can I do for you?'

Philip passed the photograph over, along with all the other paperwork.

'What do you know about this painting you've covered? Why wasn't I consulted about such a big sum insured?'

'I, I'm sorry, I was going to ask you about it, but I was told you weren't available, and it was rather urgent. They needed the cover to send the painting overseas and with such a big premium, we couldn't afford to lose it to another company.'

'I doubt another company would have taken it on. I would have been very doubtful about it myself, had I known about it.'

'I haven't seen the painting myself, all I have seen is the photograph and the details about its size and so on.'

'We are going to have to see it before we can issue a policy you know. This isn't enough on its own.'

'No, I did tell them I would need to see the painting.' Sedgewick explained.

'And what do you know about the people who valued and authenticated the painting?' demanded Philip.

'No problem there, it has been valued by a Bond Street gallery, so it will be pretty accurate. And it was authenticated by an expert,' Sedgewick said, confidently.

The gallery is in Bond Street, all right. Bond Street, Chiswick, next door to a burger bar. You've taken on a huge risk with no knowledge of the item you're covering. You idiot!'

'I say, that's a bit strong . . .'

Philip just looked at him. It was enough.

'I see what you mean, I'm terribly sorry. I suppose I was carried away by the thought of the big premium. I'll get on to checking it right away.'

'Don't bother. I've already done it. I have reason to believe the painting is a forgery and that a huge fraud is about to be perpetrated, at our expense. What do you say to that?'

Sedgewick turned a nasty shade of pale green and beads of sweat broke out on his forehead. 'What are we going to do?' he said, weakly. Philip didn't answer, he slammed the door as he left.

Julie was in Philip's office when he went in and she greeted him with her customary cheerfulness. 'Good morning, Mr Harding, it's a lovely day. How are you?'

'Uh? Oh, sorry Julie, yes, good, I mean yes, it is, I'm OK. Thanks. Can you get me a coffee and a biscuit?'

'Coming up right away, sir.' She bustled away into the little kitchen adjoining the office and reappeared after a minute or two with a tray of coffee and biscuits.

'Thank you, Julie, that's kind.'

'Not at all, are you all right, really?' asked Julie who knew him well enough to know that he was troubled by something.

'I'm sorry Julie, forgive me, it's not something I can talk about just now.'

'Whatever you say. Is there anything you need me to do?'

'No. No, I don't think so, not just now. Have you got work to do?'

'Yes, I can always find plenty to do. I'll leave you to it then, but please let me know if there is anything I can do.'

Philip's in tray was full and the day's post was neatly arranged on his desk having been opened by Julie and assessed for importance. Philip sat at his desk without a thought for his work. All he could think about was Andi and the painting insurance. Nobody had seen the painting, just the photograph, which was, no doubt, of the genuine painting. Whoever these people were, it seemed clear they were trying to set up a false claim for millions of pounds. It looked as if he was going to have to go along with it. He couldn't refuse the insurance or go to the police for fear of putting Andi in danger.

He had a sudden brainwave and picked up the phone.

'Julie? Can you see if you can get Truebright's Auctioneers on the phone for me?'

'Of course. I'll ring you back.'

Within a minute or two the phone rang.

'Truebright's for you, Mr Harding, a Mr Solomon,' Philip picked up the phone, 'Harding here, United and Overseas Insurance Company, I wonder if you can help me? I have been asked to insure a painting which I believe was sold by your company.'

'Yes, Mr Harding. What painting was that?'

'It was a Manet, an oil painting'

'Yes, I do remember such a painting, such a painting, indeed, a real beauty. How can I help you with it?'

'I understand the painting was sold for two million pounds?'

'And if it was?'

'Can you tell me who bought it?'

'I'm sorry, I can't divulge that information.'

'I understand. Well, supposing the painting, or shall we say, a painting, was sold for two million pounds, and that that was a fair price, would it be reasonable to have it insured for as much as five million?'

'Well that does seem rather a large increase, but it is quite usual to insure valuable artworks for a much higher sum than may have been paid for them. Prices are going up all the time and the value for insurance takes into consideration the cost of finding a replacement, not that it would be possible to find a replacement for a painting like this.'

'I see, thank you very much, Mr Solomon, you have been very helpful. Goodbye.'

He put down the phone and began writing on his A4 jotter pad. He listed the relevant points and studied them.

Contact Kleitner's gallery to check their valuation of the painting
Contact Fielding through the solicitors in Gloucester
Find out where the painting is being sent, and to whom.

He felt he had at least made a start and considered his next move. It would perhaps be a good idea to visit the gallery in person rather than phone. That way he could make his own judgment about their reliability. Before that though he would try to get hold of Fielding by phoning the solicitors. Once more Julie made the call for him.

'I've got a Mr Herbert Trowbridge on the phone, of Trowbridge Williams and Faulkner.' said Julie.

'Hello, Philip Harding here, United and Overseas Insurance Company. I need to get in touch with a client of yours, a Mr Percival Fielding. Can you help me?'

'Mr Fielding is out of the country at present, on business I understand.'

'Do you have an address for him? It is rather urgent.'

'I'm sorry, Sir, I have instructions not to give his address to anyone.'

'I'll tell you what it is about, then perhaps you might be a little more helpful,' Philip said with growing impatience.

'If you wish.'

'Mr Fielding has asked my company to insure a painting for him, and I need some more details. Do you know anything about a painting he bought recently?'

'We would normally act for Mr Fielding to effect any insurance he might require, using our own contacts. We are not at liberty to discuss our client's business without his authority.'

'I see, well could I ask you to pass a message to him, asking him to contact me?'

'We are not sure of Mr Fielding's exact location at present, sir, I fear we are not able to help you. Good Day.'

'Well I'm damned!' shouted Philip as he slammed down the phone. Julie, looking concerned, came into the office.

'I wish you would tell me what the trouble is Philip,' she had tried very hard to remember to call him Mr Harding when they were in the office but since they had become good friends more often than not she addressed him by his first name.

'I'm sorry, Julie, I'd like to, but it's very complicated. That fellow I just rang, he just won't help. I need to get in touch with this guy and they won't give me an address or pass on a message.'

'Philip, you know I am the soul of discretion, you can tell me what it is all about and I may even be able to help.'

'There isn't a lot I can tell you, Julie, it is all very strange. I think a fraud, quite a big one, is about to be perpetrated, but I don't know what I can do to prevent it. These people want us to insure a painting for a large sum of money. I'm not at all sure the painting is genuine, or if it is, it may not be the property of the person who wants the insurance. I'm being forced into a situation that could have very serious consequences indeed and I don't know what to do. Well, that's it in a nutshell.'

'Goodness, Philip, no wonder you are on edge.' She sat on the corner of Philips' desk and looked at him with genuine concern and affection.

'I must find that gallery,' said Philip, looking up at Julie. 'I'll go tomorrow. You can manage here can't you?'

'Of course, don't you worry. I can get hold of you on your mobile if I need to.'

'Good, that's OK then, I'll go on the train, it will be easier. I'll phone to let you know what's happening.'

Julie sensed that Philip didn't need her any more and she left the office quietly.

'What's going on?' asked Maureen from accounts, who had been hovering outside the office.

'I don't know much at all, but I do know that Philip, er, Mr Harding, is very worried. Come on I'll buy you a coffee and I'll tell you what I do know.' She took Maureen's arm and guided her to the coffee machine along the corridor.

14

"Kleitner's of Bond Street" the sign said. There was no deception, the gallery was in Bond Street, not however the famous home of Sotheby's which is of course in New Bond Street, but Bond Street off Chiswick High Street, next door to a MacDonald's. 'Clever', thought Philip as he opened the gallery's modest door.

'Good Morning, Sir.' The pretty girl sitting at a desk just inside the door looked up and smiled. 'Would you like a catalogue?'

'Not just now, thanks, I need to enquire about a painting. Who would I need to speak to?'

'Is it one of the paintings in the exhibition?'

'No, a painting that was valued by this gallery.'

'Well that would be Mr Kleitner himself then, but he is only in on Wednesdays. He spends most of his time looking for suitable works to display in the gallery. What was it you wanted to know?'

'I represent an insurance company,' he handed her his card, 'and we have been commissioned to insure the painting and I need to verify the valuation that was made before I can proceed.'

'What painting was it? I might remember it.'

'A Manet, a painting of a group of people sitting among some trees by a river.'

'We don't see many paintings of that quality here as you can imagine, so I do remember it. In fact, I think it was the first Manet I had seen, in the flesh, as it were. It was brought in for Mr Kleitner to value about a fortnight ago by a Mr, oh, what was his name, give me a minute, I will remember it, it was an unusual name – Percival Trentham-Fielding!' she recited the name grandly, 'I have never heard such a pretentious name before in my life. I knew I would remember it.' She looked delighted to have been able to come up with the information.

'That is splendid, thank you very much. Do you also happen to remember where Mr Fielding lives?'

'I put it in the diary, just a sec. Here! Percival Trentham-Fielding,' she recited again,' she smiled again.' But there is no address I'm afraid. I'm sorry.'

'Oh, pity. Never mind, thanks for your help.' As Philip made to open the door, the young lady stood up to intercept him.

'Why don't you have a look at the paintings, while you are here?'

'Thank you, I would like to, but I am in rather a hurry. Thank you so much for your help.'

So pleased was Philip to have been able to confirm the name of the elusive Fielding he was almost out of the door when he realised he had forgotten to ask where he could find Mr Kleitner.

'One more thing; what is your name by the way?'

'It's Amy, nice to meet you, Mr Harding,' she offered a delicate hand.

'It's nice to meet you too, Amy. Where can I find Mr Kleitner?'

'As I said, he comes in on Wednesdays. It's Wednesday tomorrow, you could call in and see him then,' she suggested.

'Well yes, I could, but as I said, I am in rather a hurry to get this business sorted. If I could get to see him before tomorrow it would be good.'

'He'll be out and about during the day, but you could try his flat. I've got his card here.' She picked up a card from her desk held it out. 'He lives in Chiswick, not far from the gallery.'

Philip pocketed the card and bade the helpful Amy farewell.

Having found the address by consulting his A to Z he planned to visit Mr Kleitner later in the day when he might have returned from his travels.

Mr Kleitner turned out to be a wizened little man with a wispy grey beard, not a bit what Philip had expected. He opened the door to his flat and greeted Philip in a very friendly manner.

'You'll be Mr Harding, I guess,' he said and stood aside for Philip to enter. 'How can I be of assistance?'

A few minutes later, Philip had the information he needed. The painting that Mr Kleitner had seen seemed genuine and if that were the case, it would be wise to insure it for at least five million pounds, maybe even more in the United States. Mr Kleitner was careful to qualify his opinion by saying that he could not positively state that the painting was genuine. That was not his area of expertise, although experience had taught him to sense when something was 'right'.

'So, all Fielding wanted from you was a valuation, not an authentication?'

'That's right. I told him he would have to go to an art historian or maybe someone at the National Gallery for a positive identification of the artist.'

'But you did say you thought the painting was genuine?'

'Yes, I did,'

'And did you put that opinion in writing?'

'All I said was that, to the best of my knowledge and belief, the painting was by Manet.'

'I understand. And did you charge him a fee for your valuation?'

'Oh yes indeed, I would have done it just for the pleasure of handling such a wonderful work, but business is business, you understand.'

'So, I wonder if I could ask, what name did you put on the invoice?'

'There was no invoice I'm afraid. I didn't want the money to go through the firm's books you understand,' he looked a little sheepish, 'it was a cash transaction.'

'So you don't know the name of the gentleman that brought the picture in then?'

'Well no, it was the property of a Mr Fielding, I think his name was, but I don't know the name of the man that came to see me. I'm sorry.' Kleitner looked thoughtful for a moment, 'I seem to remember hearing that Fielding lives in Gloucestershire somewhere.'

'Oh really? That's interesting. Well thank you very much, Mr Kleitner, you have been very helpful.'

Kleitner showed Philip to the door and bade him goodnight.

A few minutes after the short walk to the underground station Philip was sitting deep in thought on the tube-train to Kings Cross where he would take the train back to Peterborough.

Now having established, almost beyond doubt, that the painting was an original Manet, the property of one Trentham-Fielding, was he mistaken in thinking a fraud was being planned? No, because Andi was being forced to produce a copy.

They plan a last-minute substitution, that's it. Philip almost exclaimed aloud.

'Next stop Gloustershire', he said to himself.

It was too late to go into the office by the time he got back to Peterborough, so he picked up his car from the station car park and drove home. He phoned Darren who told him that nothing had happened his end. Philip told him what he had found out and that he was going to try to find Fielding.

'Well for goodness sake be careful, they could be dangerous.'

'I'm sure you're right Darren, I'll be careful, and I'll phone you as soon as I know anything. Are you OK? You sound awful.'

'I'm going out of my mind Philip, I don't mind telling you. But don't worry about me, I'll survive.'

Philip rang off and went into the kitchen to cobble together something to eat. He didn't feel hungry but managed to force down some cheese and crackers and large mug of black coffee.

He rang the office and told Julie that he was going to Gloucestershire to see if he could find Fielding.

'Ask Trevor to take my appointments would you, and phone me on my mobile if there is anything urgent.'

'Have you tried finding Mr Fielding on the internet?'

'What?'

'Well you can find people on the internet. Shall I try?'

'Well yes, of course, thank you Julie. Will you phone me back?'

'Of course, speak to you soon, goodbye.'

Despite working in an office with all the up to date computer equipment imaginable, Philip didn't know a great deal about computers and the internet and what it could do. He just hoped Julie was right and waited impatiently for her to phone back. It was only a few minutes before the phone rang.

'Philip? Julie. I spoke to Robert in accounts, he reckons he can find your man for you, especially as he has an unusual name.'

'Julie, that's fantastic. Why didn't you think of it before?'

'I'm sorry, it just didn't occur to me before. I'll get back to you as soon as we have something.' She rang off before Philip could say any more.

'Why on earth didn't the silly woman tell me before that she knew how to find people on the internet. She knew I was trying to find this damned Fielding fellow days ago!'

Philip shouted and stormed about his living room, getting crosser by the minute. 'We've wasted precious time on this already.' He realised he had been shouting, and stopped for a moment, trying to think if his cleaner was still in the house. He was relieved when he remembered she didn't come in on Tuesdays.

The phone rang again ten minutes later, he snatched it up.

'Yes?' he snapped.

'It's Julie, Robert has found your man, at least I think it must be him, there can't be many people with that name.'

'Oh, right, thank you, what is it then, do you have an address?' Julie read out the address and Philip wrote it down on the jotter he kept by the phone. He had calmed down a little and apologised to Julie.

'That's all right, Mr Harding,' she began. 'We all know what a strain you are under. I hope you'll be able to see this man and sort it all out. Please keep in touch.'

'Thank you, Julie, very much, and Julie, thank young Robert for me too.'

'I will, bye now, Philip.'

Philip looked at the address he had written on his note pad, "The Grange, Walton le Willows, Gloucestershire." He tore off the page and put it in his pocket, before going in search of a road atlas.

15

Walton le Willows was exactly the sort of place its name suggested, a sleepy little village that looked as if it had been conjured up by a watercolour artist. The high street was like something out of one of those old Ealing films that are sometimes shown on satellite television. Warm yellow stone cottages, some of them thatched, with jigsaw-puzzle gardens full of flowers. A little green in the centre, and next to it a church dating from around the thirteenth century, and a pub, almost as old, next door. The little village shop that also served as Post Office seemed a good place to enquire about The Grange.

There were two people waiting to be served by the elderly lady behind the glass screen of the post Office, and as might be expected there was more chat than business being done. Philip waited until he was alone in the shop before asking how to get to The Grange.

'Mr Fielding's place?' she asked? As if to say, 'why ever do you want to know where that is?'

'Yes, that's right.'

'Oh, well it's quite easy. You take the Kings Moreton road a little way then turn off where there's a sign to the Mill. There isn't a mill there any more, but nobody has bothered to take the sign down. Then just carry on along there for about a mile, I suppose it would be, and you'll see a lake on your right. Then when you have passed the lake, there'll be some trees on your left. In amongst the trees there is a turning and a sign that says, "The Grange". It is about half a mile further on. You'll see the Grange just in front of you. Are you sure you want to go there?' Philip nodded. 'Oh, well, watch out for the dogs then.'

'Thank you very much indeed, you have been very helpful.'

'Don't mention it I'm sure,' replied the lady, with an anxious expression on her face.

Back in his car, Philip consulted his map and found that the road to Kings Moreton was a continuation of the High Street. He drove slowly through the village admiring its old worldliness.

Following the directions and checking against the map he found the road marked "The Grange" and turned into the narrow entrance. The five-barred gate was open and there was nothing to suggest that visitors were not welcome, so despite the Postmistress's warning, Philip continued along the narrow tree-lined road until he saw the house a little way ahead. He had expected a grand house with a circular gravel drive in front, so was a little disappointed to find that, although very attractive and well proportioned, the house was not grand at all. In fact, had it been on an ordinary suburban road, it would hardly have merited a second glance. The setting however was magnificent. All around the house were rhododendron bushes and behind them mature trees, most of them horse chestnut, oak and elm. To the left of the house a large lawn bordered with shrubs and small trees sloped down to a small lake with an ornamental bridge. The sun was shining on the scene, making it look very desirable indeed. Philip parked the car in front of the house and walked up to the front door. He'd forgotten about the warning to watch out for the dogs, but none appeared.

He pushed the button for the bell but could not hear it ring. It either did not work or was too far from the door to be heard outside. He waited a minute before trying again. Just as he took his finger from the button, the door was opened by a tall slim man of about fifty with grey hair combed straight back, making him look severe; or was it that Philip expected him to look severe.

'Yes, can I help you?' asked the man, pleasantly enough.

'I'm looking for Mr Fielding, I'm sorry I didn't make an appointment.'

'The name is Trentham-Fielding.'

'I beg your pardon, Mr Trentham-Fielding, my name is Philip Harding, I represent the United and Overseas Insurance Company. My company has been asked to insure a painting which I understand is your property.'

'You had better come in, I think. What did you say your name was?

'Philip Harding. How do you do?' he offered his hand which Fielding took and shook briefly.

'Come through to the sitting room, would you like a cup of tea, or a glass of sherry perhaps?'

'No, thank you, you are very kind.'

'Very well, take a seat.'

They sat facing each other on identical antique sofas, separated by a large coffee table on which were scattered a selection of classy magazines.

'Now tell me, Mr Harding, you have been asked to insure a painting that belongs to me? By whom, may I ask?'

'Its all rather strange.' Philip hardly knew where to begin, 'Details were sent to my office. I don't have any names but yours, and your solicitors.'

'What is the painting, may I ask?' interrupted Fielding again.

'A Manet, a group of people sitting among trees . . .'

'Aren't they all,' muttered Trentham-Fielding, 'I should tell you before we go any further, Mr Harding, that I don't own any such painting. But do tell me more.'

'The painting was valued by an independent valuer at five million pounds . . .'

'Five million!'

'Yes, and according to the information I received, it is due to be sent to New York, on loan to a museum, and the insurance is required immediately. All I wanted to do was confirm that the painting was your property and that you had authorised its transport to New York, but if you say you don't own such a painting . . .'

'I wish I did, Mr Harding, especially if it's worth five million pounds! You say the enquiry came from my solicitors?'

'Well no, that's why I wanted to see you personally. The person that made the enquiry referred us to your solicitors, Messrs Trowbridge Williams and Faulkner of Gloucester, but they refused to discuss it when I contacted them.'

Fielding looked at Philip intently, leaning forward he clasped his hands with fingers intertwined and held them up to his mouth, resting his thumbs on his bottom lip.

'Mr Harding, I don't know how to tell you this – my solicitor's name is Brown; Herbert Brown and Partners, and their office is in Oxford. I've never heard of Trowbridge, Williams and Falkirk, or whatever you said their name was. I suspect something very funny is going on here, and you, my friend, seem to be the victim of a serious bit of shenanigans.' He released his hands and stood up.

Philip was shocked. 'But I phoned them, the solicitors I mean, and asked if they had your address.'

'What did they say?'

'That they were not at liberty to divulge your address.'

'So how did you get my address?'

'Well I tried the gallery first, where you, or should I say, someone purporting to be you, took the painting for valuation, they confirmed that a Mr Trentham-Fielding had indeed brought a painting in for valuation but didn't have your address. One of my colleagues found it in the end from the internet – he reckons he can find anyone.'

'So, this gallery – did you say which gallery?'

'Kleitners of Bond Street.'

'Really, never heard of them. They said that I had taken a painting to be valued?'

'That's right.'

'I think this could be serious, don't you?'

'I certainly do, and somehow you have become mixed up in it, Mr Trentham-Fielding.'

'It would seem so. Look, you can drop the Trentham bit, I always pile it on a bit when I don't know who I'm up against. The name is James, well it's Percival actually, but I use my second name, Percival is a family name and I dislike it intensely. May I call you Philip?'

'Of course, good to meet you, James. We seem to have been thoroughly duped by these people.

'You're telling me. What I want to know is, why me?'

'Well, I don't know. Are you involved in the art business at all?'

'I do collect paintings in a modest way, as you can see.' he waved his hand to indicate a number of paintings adorning the walls of his comfortable living room. 'My name may be known in some of the better galleries in London. Funny I haven't heard of this, what did you say it was called – Kilthams?'

'Kleitner's, it's in Bond Street but not the Bond Street everybody thinks of, that is actually New Bond Street, this one is in Chiswick.

'I see, they would need to use an obscure gallery wouldn't they, because any of the big ones would know of a painting like the Manet we are talking about. Have you seen the painting yourself?'

'No, I haven't, only a photograph of it. But I would have to see it if we are to insure it.'

'So, let me get this straight. An unidentified man contacts you to insure a painting which he claims belongs to me, but he won't tell you where I live, and won't let you see the painting, and you have a valuation from an obscure gallery in Chiswick! It's a joke surely.'

'Would that it were. I fear that it is deadly serious.'

'What was the name of the solicitors they gave you? Trowbridge, Wootton and Fellows was it?'

'Trowbridge Williams and Faulkner.'

'That's what I said; have you got their number?'

'No, I left it in the office.'

'Let's see if we can find them in the telephone book.' He got up and went to a roll-top desk in the corner of the room, rummaged for a moment and came back with two directories, sat down and began looking in the Yellow Pages. After searching for a minute or two he looked up, 'Wait a minute though, if they are insuring this painting in my name, how are they going to get hold of the money when they make their false claim, that is what they are going to do presumably.'

'Yes, I expect that's the plan. Well they have this spurious firm of solicitors, I expect the cheque would be made payable to them on your behalf. Or they could open a bank account in your name. That's the easy part.'

'I've heard of identity theft, but you never think it's going to happen to you. It's frightening isn't it?' He resumed his search then threw down the book. 'Oh, look, there clearly isn't a firm called Trowthorpe, Williams and Foxtrot, I don't know why I even looked. You have a number for them you say?

'Yes, back in the office, but I don't have an address.'

'But you will have to have an address won't you if you do this insurance for them?'

'Well yes, I would if I went ahead with it.'

'You must.'

'What do you mean, take the risk, even though the whole thing is clearly fraudulent?'

'But it's the only way we are going to nail them.'

Philip looked at James' expression and saw that he was deadly serious.

'This could cost me my job, you know.'

'Not if we make a statement and lodge it with the police, or my solicitors. Stating what has happened so far, and outlining how we are going to go about turning the tables on them.' James smiled wickedly, he was beginning to relish the situation.

'James – there is rather more to this than I have told you.' Began Philip. 'There was no need to mention it at first, but now, well . . .'

'Spit it out old chap, what's the whole story? Tell you what, I'll get us a drink and we can sit down while you tell all. What'll you have, Scotch?'

'Right oh, then yes, thanks, no water or ice.'

'Good man, that's the way I have it. I've got a drop of The Balvenie here, twelve-year-old single malt, Doublewood, don't you know, OK?'

'Couldn't be better.'

They sat down again, and Philip sipped his drink, allowing the smooth and mellow spirit to warm him before he began. He told James the whole story, right from the beginning, if not in the correct order. Their glasses were refilled several times before he had finished.

'My God, Philip, this is horrific. I don't know what to say.'

'One thing that puzzles me, James, why did the post office lady suggest I wouldn't want to come here to see you?'

James laughed. 'I am a bit of a loner, you know, a sort of recluse in a way. Oh, I have friends, but I don't mix easily, and I have built up a sort of barrier in the village by being a bit of bugger in the shops and the pub, to stop people calling in to be neighbourly. They do that here you know, and before long the whole village would be round here drinking my Scotch,' he laughed again. 'It works.'

'You seem perfectly amiable, and far from being a recluse to me, in fact I find you very easy to get on with.'

'Yes well, I have my reasons. I don't want to talk about it.'

'OK, fair enough, I won't mention it again.'

They sat drinking and chatting until late, and when Philip suggested he had better be going, James persuaded him to stay the night, as he was unfit to drive. James made some sandwiches and they sat by the fire working their way through James' malt into the early hours of the morning. They made all manner of suggestions how they might foil the insurance fraudsters but every time it came back to the question of Andi.

'When you said we would turn the tables on the crooks, what did you have in mind?' asked Philip, as James was pouring himself another shot of his favourite Doublewood.

'Well, I didn't have anything specific in mind, but I thought perhaps we could put a trace on the painting somehow and make sure they didn't destroy it, or if they claimed it had been stolen, we could find it and give it back to them. Then you wouldn't have to pay out on the insurance. Something like that.'

'Oh, I see. Nothing very practical then,' said Philip disappointed. But he smiled as he held up his own glass for another dram.

Philip drove straight to Andi's flat after leaving Walton le Willows the following morning. He'd promised to keep James in the picture.

'Any news, Darren?' he called as he entered the flat.

'Nothing. I don't know what to do. Do you think I should stay here?'

'It wouldn't be a bad idea, in case she comes back. On second thoughts, she'll have our numbers if she's able to call, so you don't have to stay here.'

'I think I'll be happier staying here, Philip, if you don't mind.'

'I don't mind, of course. I'll know where to find you if anything happens. I've got to go back to Peterborough now, but I'll come back later if I can. Whatever happens, I'll keep in touch. OK?'

'Yeah, you get off. I'll see you later.'

'I'll tell you all about the mysterious Mr Trentham-Fielding when I get back.

'Oh yes, I'd forgotten you were going to find him. I'm all agog.'

'You'll have to wait, I'm afraid, I must get back to the office. Bye.'

16

Two weeks had passed, and Andi had worked hard and long on the Manet. Now it was finished, and she was pleased with it, despite the circumstances, but now she had fulfilled her obligation, what would Beaumont do with her? She dared not think. She must try to escape.

She tried the door again. It was a Yale type lock and securely latched. She knew that the credit card trick was no more than a fiction, but nevertheless thought she might be able to push the latch back with a suitable tool. She looked for something she could use. The workbench was equipped with a range of implements an artist might use, including several palette knives. Andi picked one up and tested the blade against her hand. It was strong and not too flexible. The door opened inwards, so she could see the flat side of the latch in the gap between the door and the frame. By levering the catch and pulling the door against it to prevent it from sliding back, levering it again, and pulling the door to hold it, several times, the catch was fully retracted. She just had to turn the handle and pull the door a little way towards her. She reached round and snibbed the latch so that it would not lock again. With the door open enough for her to look out, she stood and listened – there was no sound from below and no light showed up the stairs. She went back into the room and picked up her coat and crept, as quietly as she could, down the stairs.

There was still no sound from the room downstairs and no light showed under the door. She made for the front door, turned the knob of the Yale lock.

It was almost completely dark and there was a cold wind that made her pull her flimsy coat tight around her. She walked a little way along the drive and looked back at the house. The studio lights were still on, but no other light showed. They really had left her alone.

Feeling elated, having escaped, Andi quickened her pace as she walked along the drive. She had no idea where she was but thought she would be able to find her way home somehow.

She reached the end of the drive and found herself on a narrow road with high hedges. Nothing could be seen beyond the road and there was no sound. She had a feeling they had turned right into the drive when she had been brought here so she turned left, hoping to retrace the route they had taken in the car.

A steep hill soon after leaving the house made walking hard work and after perhaps half an hour Andi began to feel anxious. She didn't seem to be getting anywhere. She hadn't seen any sign of life and the lane was eerily quiet. Thinking that civilisation might lie in the opposite direction, she turned around and retraced her steps, all the time worried that her captors might return and find her missing, she took great care when she reached the house. The lane continued past the house, but it was much narrower, and Andi began to think it was not leading to habitation of a kind that might offer her assistance. Her captors would come looking for her and there was nowhere to hide.

After a few hundred yards, the lane opened up onto an area that might have been a car-park, but there were no cars and no sign indicating its purpose. A neglected-looking post box was built into to the stone wall. She walked on. The surface of the road was covered with sand and there were narrow tracks that might have been made by a very small car. There was a slight breeze to begin with but as the road took a downward slope the wind became stronger and ruffled Andi's hair. She shivered as she stood listening. A faint watery sound suggested she was near the sea.

This was quite unexpected; she was obviously much further from home than she had thought. There were no buildings to be seen, no sign of life at all. The chances of finding her way home from here were as remote as the location. She walked on, getting nearer to the sound of the sea.

Away from any source of artificial light, the sky did not seem completely dark; there were stars and a half moon that gave a surprising amount of light. She was able to see quite well.

The road came to an abrupt end and only a narrow path continued in the same direction. Andi tentatively continued, the sound of the sea getting louder all the time.

A short flight of steps led down to a stone flagged path facing a small bay. The moon shone on the water. Small waves lapped the beach. Along one side of the bay stood a row of wooden beach huts. They had been painted in pastel colours many years ago and most of the paint had peeled off revealing worn and weathered timbers. Andi climbed the half dozen steps up to the wooden walkway in front of the huts and tried the doors as she walked along. There were about a dozen huts in various states of disrepair. She thought how nice it would be to sit in one of these huts in the summer, looking out at what would undoubtedly be a lovely view.

The door of the fourth hut was not locked. She opened it and peered inside. It was too dark to see anything clearly, but she could just make out a couple of deckchairs and a small bed. She couldn't hope to find her way home until it got light so perhaps she could rest here. She crept inside and pulled the door to behind her. Taking care not to bang into anything she made for the bed and sat down. Out of the wind it was quite warm inside the hut and the previous occupiers had kindly left a rug on the bed. She lay down and soon slept.

17

Darren had taken time off from his part-time work at a wholesale couturiers as soon as Andi disappeared, but as it seemed there was nothing useful he could do in the search for Andi, he rang his firm to see if there was anything for him.

He had always fancied himself as a fashion designer so the job at the wholesale couturier interested him although his job was little more than delivery driver and odd job man. Delivering dresses to retailers meant he could see lots of beautiful clothes and the proximity to so many fine gowns inspired him. Sometimes he was able to work on the dresses himself, doing minor repairs. He was able to study the work of top designers and seamstresses, learning as he did. One day, he thought, he would get his chance.

One evening, soon after Philip had returned to Peterborough, Darren was loading the company van with a consignment of wedding dresses for a big shop in Brighton. A man standing in the shadow by the warehouse door, called his name. Thinking it must be one of the firm's staff, he walked over.

As he entered the shadow, blows came hard and fast, vicious punches to his solar plexus put him down on his knees, gasping for air, kicks to his ribs and kidneys finished him. Everything went dark, there was no more pain.

Gordon, the warehouse manager, realising that the back doors were still open, and the van was still standing in the alley, went to investigate.

'Darren! My God! What has happened? Oh, you're hurt. Here, let me help you.'

But Darren was unconscious and there was nothing Gordon could do. He looked up and down the alley but there was nobody there. He quickly closed the van doors and went back to his little office to phone for an ambulance.

Philip had been unable to contact Darren. He'd texted as usual, just to keep in touch, as he always did while in Peterborough, but when there was no reply he tried phoning. Darren's phone was switched off.

'He wouldn't switch it off, surely,' thought Philip, 'he knows we need to keep in touch. Something must be wrong.'

It was not possible for Philip to leave the office as there was a training day for staff in which he was heavily involved.

He phoned the police and asked to speak to Inspector Wallace, with whom they had spoken about Andi's disappearance.

'Have you heard from Mr Wilson?' asked Philip, without preamble when the phone was answered.

'I'm sorry, sir, what is this in connection with?'

'Sorry, my name is Harding, Philip Harding, of the United and Overseas Insurance Company . . .'

'Yes, sir, and?'

'Don't you remember me? We are investigating the disappearance of Miss Pertell.'

'Oh, yes, sir, there's no news I'm afraid. We'll let you know if we find her.'

'Hopeless,' said Philip, under his breath.

'What was that, sir?'

'I want to report another missing person, Mr Darren Wilson . . .'

'Another one, Mr Harding, you really must be more careful with your friends.'

'I don't like your attitude, Inspector, this is serious!'

'I'm sorry, sir, yes of course. Give me the details. I assure you we do take cases of missing persons seriously, but so often the people are not missing at all, or they've chosen to disappear. We waste a lot of time looking for them.'

'Yes, I understand. I'll tell you about Mr Wilson.'

Philip told the policeman all he could, which was not very much, that made him think something was seriously wrong. The inspector, after apologising for his levity, noted all the details and assured Philip that the police would do all they could.

18

Fearing for Darren's safety, Philip phoned all the local hospitals, but no Darren Wilson had been admitted. He asked people in Darren's known haunts if they had any news of him, but it was only when he thought to contact the fashion house where Darren worked part-time, that he was able to find out what had happened. He learned of the brutal attack and his serious injuries. Darren had been taken by ambulance to the Accident and Emergency department of the nearest hospital. There had been no news of his condition since.

Because Darren had been unconscious when admitted to hospital and had nothing on him to identify him, the name Darren Wilson had not been recognised.

Dropping everything, Philip drove down to London and found the one remaining parking space at the hospital.

When Philip described, as best he could, the circumstances of Darren's admission, the receptionist was able to direct him to a ward where an unidentified man was being treated.

The ward sister listened to Philip's anxious enquiry and concluded that her patient might well be Philip's friend. He was shown to a bed hidden behind flowery curtains.

Darren was festooned with tubes and wires and a machine next his bed bleeped at regular intervals. His face was covered with bruises and his head was bandaged. A drip with a bag of clear liquid was connected to his arm. He appeared to be unconscious.

Philip approached the bedside cautiously and whispered Darren's name.

There was no response. He tried again, 'Darren, old friend, it's Philip.'

The nurse, who had shown Philip to Darren's bed, touched him gently on his arm and said she didn't think Darren could hear.

'I'm afraid your friend is very badly injured, Mr Harding. Best let him rest. You can phone as often as you like to find out of there has been any change, but for the time being you can rest assured he is getting the best treatment.' She smiled and led Philip away from the bed, adjusting the curtains as she did so.

Horrified at the sight of his new friend, Philip left the hospital in something of a daze. Was this attack connected with the paintings and Andi's kidnapping? It seemed the most likely explanation, but if so, it had become deadly. He had not considered Andi's life to be in danger because they, whoever they were, needed her to paint the fake pictures, but now . . .

Philip concluded that the villains had found out about Darren's investigations and had sought to stop him. They had clearly got too close to their operation. Philip now feared for his own safety.

Philip went to the police station. Better to appear in person he thought. Once more requesting to see the inspector he had spoken to before, he was shown into an interview room. He didn't have to wait long before the inspector entered.

'Inspector Wallace,' Philip began, 'I have news of Mr Wilson. He has been very badly injured in an attack and is now lying unconscious in hospital . . .'

'Oh, yes, your missing friend, we had notification of an unidentified person being admitted to hospital after an attack. So what can you tell me?'

'Not much at all, I'm afraid, other that Mr Wilson is very poorly indeed. I fear the attack was made by the people I told you about. The whole thing has now become much more serious.'

'Yes, yes, I see that, I do see that, of course. Well thank you for letting me know. Leave it with me, I will have an officer posted to Mr Wilson's bedside so that we can find out what happened as soon as he regains consciousness.'

Accepting that there was little more the inspector could promise at this stage, Philip got up, ready to leave.

'Be very careful, Mr Harding, if what you have told me is true, and the attack on Mr Wilson was connected with this kidnapping and fraud business, you could be in danger yourself.'

'Yes, thanks for that, Inspector!' Philip allowed himself a grim smile, shook the inspector's hand and left the station.

He headed back to the company's head office.

19

Philip was greeted enthusiastically by the receptionist in the lobby. 'Hello, Mr Harding, nice to see you. Can I help you at all?'

'No, that's Okay, Sandra. Is the boss in?'

'Mr Maltby? Yes, he has just gone up to his office as a matter of fact. Would you like me to tell him you are here?'

'Yes, perhaps you had better, he doesn't like surprise visits. Ask him if it is okay for me to come up.'

Mr Maltby was happy for Philip to go straight up so he took the executive lift to the top floor.

'Philip, my boy! Come on in, what a nice surprise. Have a seat. Can I get you a drink? Have you decided on a car, yet? You need to get a car, it shows the customers we are a successful company, you know.'

'What? Oh, sorry, yes, I got a Jaguar, an XK8, but I haven't had very much opportunity to drive it yet. Look, I don't want a drink, I need to talk to you about a rather worrying situation . . .' Philip sat on one of the two antique chairs in front of Maltby's desk.

'Goodness, well, you'd better tell me then.'

'I don't know where to begin. This is about as serious as it could be . . .'

'I can see this is worrying you. You did right to come to me with your concerns. Let me be the judge. Just tell me what it is.'

'A fraud is about to be carried out and the company is heavily involved . . .

Maltby got up from his seat behind his enormous desk and ushered Philip to the comfortable seats by the window.

'Go on.'

Leaning forward, Philip began to explain. 'It came to my notice that some paintings have been forged and passed off as originals and it appears that we, that is the company, has been asked to provide insurance cover for at least one of them which is being shipped to the States.'

'I see. This is serious Philip. What do you suggest we do?'

'I don't know. I don't want to accuse anyone without more information, but I don't want it to go any further if I am right.'

'What, do you mean someone in the company is involved in the fraud?'

'I'm not sure, but as I see it, it does look that way.'

'If we have been asked to insure something that is part of a fraud, that doesn't mean we are guilty of fraud, just that we have been used. A different matter entirely,' said Maltby, relaxing a little.

'Yes, I see that. But I think someone in the firm is involved with the perpetrators. I can't prove it, but it does look suspicious.'

'You must tell me all you know, and what you suspect, Philip, if we are to get to the bottom of this. Have we issued a policy, do you know?'

'If we haven't already, a policy is in the process of being issued.'

'We need to stop it. We can always reissue if it turns out you are wrong. But you must tell me who you think is involved.'

'I am reluctant to name names you understand . . .'

'Yes, yes, I do understand, but in the circumstances you must let me deal with this.'

'I am not accusing him of anything at this stage, but the person dealing with the insurance is Stewart Sedgewick. I am not saying he is responsible for the fraud – if that's what it is – but he did bring in details of a painting that his client wants to insure and which I believe to be a forgery. What I don't know is if he took the business, knowing it to be fraudulent.'

'Why do you think the painting is a forgery?'

'Because I know who painted it. At least I think she painted it.'

'Who is this person? And can't you ask her if she painted the picture?'

'She is a friend of mine; her name is Andrea Pertell. She is a picture restorer, but she paints copies of paintings for clients who want to keep the originals in safety deposits.'

'Oh yes, I know about that, in fact I had a copy made of one of my own valuable paintings that is now kept at my bank, but are you saying she paints the odd forgery as well?'

'She wouldn't call the paintings she does forgeries, as they were not signed and as far as she was aware, to begin with at least, they would never be passed off as originals. But then she was asked to sign the paintings and make them as much like the originals as possible.

She spoke to me about it because she was worried that they might be passed off as originals.'

'And why can't you just ask her about this particular painting, did you say?'

'Because she is missing. '

'Missing – what do you mean?'

'She was supposed to come to my party but didn't turn up, and I haven't been able to find her since. I think she has been forced to paint forgeries and is being held somewhere.'

'Are you sure you are not jumping to conclusions?'

'No, I have no doubt, I have evidence that suggests very clearly what has happened to her, I just don't know where she is being held.'

'My God, Philip. Have you informed the police?'

'Yes, I have. They weren't very interested until I told them a fraud was being carried out.'

'Let me get this straight. Why do you think Sedgewick is involved? He could have simply been asked to insure the painting and brought the business in quite innocently.'

'He could, but there are some interesting reasons why that doesn't look right to me. First, Sedgewick recently asked to be transferred to the Peterborough branch – my branch. It is common knowledge that my girlfriend is an art restorer, so he would know about Andi. That in itself is not enough, but I saw him at an art auction a day or two ago, and he was selling a very valuable painting which I am pretty sure was also painted by my friend. Here's what I think their plan is. They try to get the insurance in the normal way, but if we, or more specifically, I am suspicious and refuse to provide cover, they bring in their big guns – the fact that they have Andi held captive. They will force me to do the business – or else. I think this has been very carefully set up over a period of some weeks or months. Sedgewick moving to Peterborough was the first step.'

Maltby looked long and hard at Philip before answering.

'Oh, Dear, Philip, I am most dreadfully sorry – I have used you badly. I'll explain, but you must promise me, this must not go out of this office, you understand?'

'Of course.'

'Well, Sedgewick and I go back a long way, we were up at Cambridge together, rowing blues and all that – you understand? Well, a little while ago, Sedgewick wrote a policy on some very expensive jewellery, big premium you understand, then they, the jewels were stolen, or they disappeared. They were never recovered, and we had to pay out. It was one of the biggest payouts the company has ever had to make. There was nothing to suggest any fraud, or anything like that, it was just unfortunate. But then, not long afterwards, Sedgewick wrote a policy on a very rare historic Ferrari motor car, eleven million pounds. You can imagine the premium. I cautioned Sedgewick at the time, but he said it was kosher and the car was safely tucked up in a museum, so it went through. You can guess, I expect, what happened. There was a devastating fire, and the car, along with several others that were insured by another firm, was totally destroyed. The assessors examined the burnt out remains and said it was the car in question. So we paid out again. It could have finished a smaller company. On top of the jewels, it very nearly finished us. So, although I had no reason to suspect Sedgewick of dirty dealings or anything like that, I had him moved to Peterborough out of the way, while I got some people in to examine his books, just to be sure, you understand.'

'I was going to ask you why he moved to Peterborough before all this blew up,' said Philip. 'So, what did the people find, if anything?'

'Nothing at all. Everything seemed as right as rain. I had no reason to doubt Sedgewick's honesty. But then you come along with this nightmare. I don't know what to think.'

'What did Sedgewick have to say about you investigating his books?'

'Oh, I didn't tell him. I spun him a story about him being useful in the new office, and he swallowed it. I felt guilty about it. I am not a devious man, you understand, but I had to be sure.'

'Of course,' Philip agreed.

'So, I am sorry I misled you, Philip. It was just that I had to keep it as quiet as possible.'

'I would not have said a word about it, David,' said Philip, a little hurt at not being consulted.

'Of course you wouldn't, as I say, I am very sorry. But now, what are we going to do about this new problem?'

Maltby looked away for a moment, then turned to Philip. 'You must allow the insurance to go ahead, Philip, whatever it costs. We can't put your lady-friend in danger.'

'But it could cost the company millions, Sir. I mean David.'

'That's a risk we're going to have to take. But if we are careful, or clever, we might be able to get away with it. Any ideas?'

20

Philip didn't have any ideas and left Maltby with the promise that he would try to come up with something.

Back in Peterborough several hours later, Philip was catching up on day to day business with Julie.

'If that's all then, Julie, and you can sort out the routine stuff, I'm going to have another word with our friend Sedgewick. Extension 230 if you need to get in touch.'

'Right you are, Phi – I mean Mr Harding.'

Philip smiled as he left the office.

He took the lift and walked along the corridor towards Sedgewick's office, not knowing what he was going to say, but pushed open the door confidently and strode in. Sedgewick looked up and seeing Philip's expression, paled noticeably.

'Good morning, Mr Harding,' he began, standing awkwardly behind his desk. 'How can I help you?'

'Sit down, Sedgewick. I want to ask you some questions. If you don't tell me what I want to know I am going to hand you over to the police and tell them of the fraud you are trying to carry out.'

'I don't know what you are talking about,' said Sedgewick, still standing, but gripping the edge of his desk.

'It's no good, Sedgewick. I know all about it.'

Sedgewick's face lost all its colour and he struggled to remain standing. Sweat broke out on his forehead.

'You had better sit down, before you fall down, you wimp!'

Sedgewick sat. He seemed to have shrunk, his eyes wide with fright.

'Now,' said Philip. Still standing, he had the advantage of height and could look down at Sedgewick. 'You are going to tell me all you know.'

'I can't tell you anything. I don't know anything,' he bleated.

'I don't believe you. You are making a lot of money from your dodgy dealings, Sedgewick, but it's over. You are going to tell me everything.' Philip had never been in a situation like this, his mouth was dry and he could feel his heart beating. But he was in command of the moment and determined to win.

'I daren't say anything.'

'What do you mean—you daren't say anything? You had better tell me, Sedgewick. I don't care if you are a friend of the boss. He's told me a lot about you, already.'

'No, I know the boss has me under investigation, it's not that. There are other people involved. I daren't say anything, I tell you. I just daren't.'

'What do you know about the art forgery?'

Sedgewick looked horrified, how could Philip know about that?

'Yes, I know about that, too. So you'd better tell me all you know, and the names of the people involved.'

'Look, I'm sorry, I don't know how you know what you know, but believe me, it is dangerous to start looking into it.'

'I have started looking into it, and I know a lot already, but I need to know more.' Philip was wondering if he dare mention Andi. Did Sedgewick know anything about her, and her whereabouts? He decided to risk it.

'Where is Miss Pertell being held?'

'What?'

'You heard.'

'I don't know anything about Miss, what did you say her name was?'

'I think you do, Sedgewick, and I am getting impatient.' Philip's voice rose, and he leaned across Sedgewick's desk and grabbed the terrified man's lapels. 'Tell me where she is!'

'I can't tell you what I don't know, I am not part of the organisation. They don't tell me anything.'

'But you do know that Andi—Miss Pertell is working for them, don't you?' He pushed the terrified man back into his seat and leaned on the desk.

Sedgewick didn't answer.

'Don't you!' Philip shouted.

'Well, I know she has done some paintings for them,' Sedgewick admitted, weakly.

'So where is she? She is not at home and I have reason to believe she is being held against her will and made to paint forgeries.'

Sedgewick's expression was enough for Philip to be convinced he knew something about Andi's whereabouts.

'Oh, so you do know about that, do you? So, where is she?'

'Oh, I don't know that. I had nothing to do with that – you've got to believe me, it wasn't my idea. But, yes, all right, I did know about it. You can't turn me in. They'll know that you are on to them and I dread to think what they might do.'

'Miss Pertell is far too valuable for them to harm her, so I have no worries about that. I want to know where she is being held, and I suspect you know more than you make out. I'm getting impatient, Sedgewick, if you tell me all you know, I might ask the police to be lenient.'

'I couldn't help it, Mr Harding, they had me over a barrel. They forced me to help them. I didn't think it was all that serious at first, and by the time I saw how much trouble I was in, it was too late.'

'Go on, I'm listening. Tell all,' said Philip, pulling a chair close to Sedgewick's.

Sedgewick was sweating, he took out a large handkerchief and mopped his forehead. He looked terrified, as if his co-conspirators might burst into the room at any minute.

'You see, I'm quite a keen art collector. I can't afford to buy the good stuff, but I go to all the sales and I see all these beautiful paintings being sold to people who just want them as investments. They lock them up in vaults, Mr Harding! Where nobody can see them. I wanted them, Mr Harding. I wanted to hang them on my walls and admire them. That's what they are for, to look at and admire, don't you see?'

'Yes, I do, so, what did you do?'

'I asked Miss Pertell to make a copy of a particularly desirable oil painting that was coming up for sale at Kleitners . . .'

'Oh, it was you that got her into this was it! By God, Sedgewick, I should give you a bloody good hiding!'

Philip stood up, shaking with anger, and leaned over Sedgewick, his fists clenched.

'I'm sorry,' gasped Sedgewick, fearing that Philip was going to hit him. 'I didn't want to get her into trouble. I just wanted a copy, that's all. Anyway, when I saw the painting Miss Pertell produced, it was so good, I thought it would pass as an original and it gave me an idea. I devised a plan to switch the paintings at the auction. The real painting would go into the sale, but when the customer came to collect it, it would be my copy. It was easy. There was no security in the storeroom at the rear of the auction house. I just walked in and switched the paintings. Nobody saw me. Nobody was hurt by it. The fool who had bought the picture couldn't have told the difference and the painting would be put in a vault somewhere.'

'And when the poor unsuspecting buyer comes to cash in on his investments, when he retires perhaps, he'll find out that his pension is going to be a lot less. Not very nice.'

'No, well, I expect he's got pots of money anyway. A lot more than me anyway. OK, I know it was wrong, but you have to agree, not very serious.'

'I'm not sure that I agree with you. What you did was fraud, and theft. I don't know what you will be done for, Sedgewick, but you will go to prison, that's for sure. How long, will depend on how much you can tell me about these people who are trying to defraud the company. I believe there's a thing called Queen's Evidence, it could save you quite a bit of time in one of Her Majesty's rest homes.'

'They'd kill me, Mr Harding, you don't know them, they are real full-time professional villains.'

'Tell me the rest of the story.'

'Oh, well. After I had been successful with the switch I got greedy. I studied the catalogues of the smaller auction houses to find paintings that I liked and when I found something suitable, I asked Miss Pertell to make me a copy.'

'How long has this been going on? Demanded Philip.

'About a year I suppose,'

'And how many paintings did An . . . I mean Miss Pertell, copy for you?'

'Six.'

'And where are they?'

'Who knows, with the people who bought them, in some bank vault I expect.'

'I meant the ones you stole.'

'In my flat.'

'Hidden?'

'No, of course not. I told you, I want to be able to see the paintings. They are hanging on the walls. They are wonderful, Mr Harding, you should see them.'

'The sad thing is that in all probability they will finish up in vaults after all, when they have been recovered and returned to their rightful owners. The copies will be destroyed, and you'll be in prison. You could have been enjoying those very clever copies – you said yourself they were virtually indistinguishable from the originals. Do please go on, I am intrigued to hear the next part of your story.'

'Well, I got caught. The last one I was a bit careless with. One of the auction porters saw me bringing my copy into the store-room and challenged me. There was nothing I could do. It was obvious even to him, what I was up to. He threatened to call the police at first but then he decided to tell some mates of his. That's how I got involved with these heavy crooks. They said If I helped them they wouldn't go to the police. The porter hadn't told his bosses, so the switches had still gone unreported.'

'So what did they want you to do?'

'Ironically, it was my scam that gave them the idea. They thought they could pull a switch themselves, only on a much bigger scale. They would get a copy made of a very valuable painting and get it insured, and then somehow it would disappear and they would claim for it. Easy money. By now they had made contact with Miss Pertell – I had to tell them who had made the copies – and they made her agree to paint the copy or they would report her for the copies she had made for me. You see, we were both involved inextricably and there was nothing we could do.'

'I see. And when did all this happen?' asked Philip, who was by now so interested in Sedgewick's story, he had almost forgotten to be angry with him.

'It was just after you had been made manager of this branch, and people were transferring from head office. I didn't want to move, myself. I'm a Londoner, through and through. I don't like the countryside. It was the boss who wanted me to move up to Peterborough, but it suited me because I thought I would be safer up here. But the guy in charge of the villains got to hear of the move. I told you, he already knew of your relationship with Miss Pertell. He thought I would be in an even better position to set up the insurance in a provincial branch, you see.'

'So you've been planning this for over a year!' exclaimed Philip. Like a time-bomb, you could say.'

And then, when the significance of what Sedgewick had just said had sunk in – 'You thought we'd be a bit thick out in the sticks and would be less likely to suspect something dodgy – is that what you thought?

'I'm so sorry, Mr Harding, I really am, but you see now, I had no choice. I'm willing to help you all I can, but I don't know what can be done. If I don't write the policy for the painting, well, I dread to think what they might do . . .'

'Yes, yes, I see that, shut up a minute, and let me think.'

21

Philip left Sedgewick's office in slightly better mood than he'd been in when he entered it. Sedgewick had cleared up one or two points, but had raised a few more. Philip needed to think. And he needed someone to help him. With Darren out of action, the only person he could think of was James Fielding.

'Hello, James,' Philip said, when the phone was answered. 'Can I come over, I need to talk things over and you are the only person who can help.'

'Of course, dear boy, come on over, I'm almost always here, and I've replenished my stock of good whisky!'

'I'll be with you in a couple of hours then, goodbye.' Philip hung up and looked at his watch. It was already late afternoon, but he needed to see James as soon as possible. He quickly told Julie where he was going and left the office.

Choosing to go via Kettering, Coventry and Stratford, because he reckoned that route would have less traffic, and as he was still unused to his new car, it actually took almost three hours to get to Walton le Willows. It was eight o'clock when he rang James' door bell.

'I'm so sorry it is so late, James,' began Philip. But James was smiling and brushed aside the apology.

'I'm glad of the company, don't worry. Have a seat, I'll get you a drink.' he said, ushering Philip into his comfortable book-lined living room. A cheerful log fire burned in the large fireplace.

Philip sat in a comfortable wing armchair by the fire, enjoying the rich comfort of the room.

'Have you eaten?' said James, handing a generously filled tumbler of whisky to Philip.

'No, I seemed to have lost track of time today.'

'Then I will cook, and you can tell me what it is that's bothering you while we eat. How does pork medallions with runner beans and new potatoes sound?'

'That sounds absolutely wonderful. I haven't eaten properly for days.'

Less than an hour later they were sitting down to eat, washing down the pork with a nice bottle of Zinfandel.

'Can you talk and eat, dear boy?' James asked as they began to eat?'

'I shall have to, James, I need to sort this out as soon as possible. I've told you the situation, all about the forged paintings and Andi's kidnap, so we needn't go over that. My problem now is to get to see the painting they plan to ship to the States just before it is packed to go, to make sure it is the real thing. You see I'm pretty sure they plan to switch the paintings at the last minute.'

'Yes, I see, more wine?'

'OK, thanks, do you see my problem?'

'Yes, indeed. But once you have established the genuine painting is the one you are insuring, isn't that sufficient?'

'No, because I think they plan to switch the paintings, stow the original somewhere, or even return it to its rightful owner, then, somehow either lose the bogus canvas or destroy it, and then claim on the insurance. They will make sure it is not possible to tell whatever remains was the fake.'

'It hardly seems worth the bother,' mused James.

'When you consider the painting is insured for five million pounds, you will agree that it is worth the bother – and the risk.'

'Oh, yes, of course, I see what you mean. So how do you propose to keep tabs on the thing, so to speak?'

Philip chewed pensively for a moment.

'That is where I hope you can help me, James.'

After they had finished their meal, which Philip said was the best he'd had for a long time, they sat drinking James' whisky, and by the end of the evening they had come up with a plan.

For the first time in weeks, Philip went to bed feeling a little better. This might just work.

22

Andi was woken by the harsh cries of seagulls and just for a moment she could not identify the sound. Light shone feebly through the flimsy curtains of the beach hut. She went to the window and pulled the curtain a little to one side. There appeared to be nobody about. It was only eight o'clock and not yet fully light. If there were people living in the area they would perhaps not be about yet. For the moment she felt safe where she was, but she would have to move before long. She sat down again and tried to think what to do. She was hungry and thirsty. The hut was well equipped for summer habitation, with all the paraphernalia of seaside holidays. There was a bucket and spade, a kite, a windbreak, several folding deckchairs, stacked up on the back wall, and a cupboard with a drop-down front on which stood a little bottle-gas stove and a kettle. With trembling hands Andi opened the cupboard door. Inside were tins of tea and coffee, sugar, even powdered milk, but no matches to light the stove. A large plastic container on the floor must surely contain water. She bent to pick it up and shook it. A row of colourful mugs hung from hooks inside the cupboard and soon she was drinking rather stale tasting water and wishing she had the means to light the stove. A cup of coffee would have been wonderful. Further investigation of the interior of the cupboard revealed a tin of stale ginger biscuits and a jar of marmalade. The biscuits would suffice for the time being, but she would need something more substantial before long. It was a long time since her last meal.

Somewhat fortified by her stolen breakfast, Andi ventured outside. It was cold but sheltered from the wind by the high cliffs. The bay was, as she had imagined, beautiful. It would be a perfect spot in which to spend a summer holiday. The tide had gone out, revealing a swathe of beautiful pale golden sand. The cliffs on the far side of the bay were a blaze of colour where the sun had begun to work its way down. Seabirds wheeled and mewed – appearing, Andi thought, to laugh at her predicament. But, however beautiful, it was dangerously close to Andi's erstwhile prison, and she had to get away as quickly as she could.

Walking back the way she had come the night before, she found the car park again, still empty. She walked back along the lane a little way to see if there were any houses where she might get help. But there was nothing and nobody. She could begin to walk back as far as she could guess the way they had come the evening before and hope to be able to thumb a lift, but she might have to walk a long way before she saw a car. She saw the post box in the wall and had the beginnings of an idea. It would mean going back to the house and risking the consequences of absconding if the men had returned, but what could they do. They couldn't hurt her; they needed her to paint. She strode back towards the house, slowing apprehensively when she got near. The drive was still empty. The car was not there. Did that mean they had not returned, or that the car had brought the men back and then gone away? She had to risk it.

The front door of the house was unlocked. Had she left it unlocked last night? She could not remember. She went in. All was quiet. She crept up the stairs. The door to the studio was open. She went in. Empty. She realised that she had been holding her breath and now relaxed. She was still alone. But they had said they would feed her, so it would not be long before someone came with food. She would have to hurry. The post box had given her an idea. She had seen a Polaroid camera on the desk – artists often used Polaroids. If she took a photograph of the house, or perhaps the beach huts and the bay would be better, and sent it to Philip, he would be able to identify it and come and rescue her. It was a long shot, but she could think of nothing better. It would take time of course and if she hid in the beach hut until such time as Philip was able to find her, she would be very hungry indeed.

Should she wait for someone to come with food and hope they go away again? If they stayed, she wouldn't be able to take the photograph and post it. She decided to risk it.

If only they would leave food for her and leave, she would again make her escape . . .

It struck her that maybe there was food in the house. She hadn't attempted to explore before for fear of being caught, but if the men were out of the house she could look for food in the kitchen.

There were three rooms downstairs. The living room, sparsely furnished in 1930s style, with a garishly patterned carpet, armchairs and a settee with big rounded arms, and a small bookcase with a selection of very old Penguin paperbacks. The dining room, with a table and four chairs, also dating from before the second world war. Trechikov's 'Green Chinese Woman', hanging over the tiled fireplace was the one attempt at decoration.

The kitchen, at the back of the house was another piece of history. The electric cooker must have been one of the first of its kind, and the enamel topped table was like the one Andi remembered seeing in her great grandmother's house. A green painted cabinet of nineteen-thirty vintage was the only piece of furniture and the possible source of food. Andi pulled down the flap at the front to reveal several shelves which were completely empty. She pulled open the drawer and found treasure of a sort – a box of matches. She would be able to make herself a cup of coffee in the beach hut. All she needed was some bread or a tin of soup – anything to keep her going until Philip was able to identify the picture and come to her rescue.

Just as she was about to give up she noticed a rubbish bin in the corner. Only desperation would cause her to investigate it for possible sustenance, but she was desperate. A polythene bag contained half a loaf of sliced bread. The bread was still quite soft but there were a few specks of mould on the edges of the slices that would normally have caused Andi to dump the bread, but she thought the crusts could be cut off. She vaguely remembered hearing that it was not safe to eat mouldy bread, even if you cut off the actual mould, but she had no choice. She looked in the drawer again and found a knife and a spoon. She put all her finds into the polythene bag and after looking round once more, decided to return to the beach hut.

She eased open the front door to see if there was any sign of the return of her captors, and left the house, keeping well to the side of the drive so that if she heard a car she could dodge behind a tree. When she reached the end of the drive, she peered cautiously out on to the road, looking both ways for any sign of a car. There was nothing, not a soul.

Looking behind her every few steps, she hurried back to the beach hut and comparative safety. She reasoned that even if the men came looking for her when they discovered she had gone, it would take a long time before they thought to look here. They would assume she would make her way along the road, back the way they came.

She put her treasures in the hut and went to find a good vantage point from which to take her Polaroid photograph. She took several shots and went back to the hut to decide which seemed the best to identify the bay. She then wrote a simple message on the back and addressed the photograph to Philip's company. She didn't have a stamp. But felt sure the post office would deliver it and claim the postage from the company.

Praying that the post-box was still in service, she pushed her precious postcard through the slot.

She now had enough food to keep her going for a while, she had the means to make a hot drink and somewhere safe to hide. She settled down to wait.

23

Philip decided to speak to Sedgewick again, but this time he was wanting his cooperation, so did not show the anger which still simmered.

'When is the painting due to be shipped out to the States?'

'I'm not sure about that, but I do know they want the insurance cover to start from the first of next month.'

'What arrangements have been made to see the painting before it is packed up to travel?'

'None yet. I was waiting to hear from them.'

'Because you realise that whatever pressures are being made against you to produce the policy, nothing can be done until we have seen the painting and confirmed that it is in fact the genuine article.'

'But I thought you said they were going to substitute the real painting with the one that Miss Pertell is doing?'

'I think you knew that yourself, but yes, that is, I'm sure what they plan to do. However, we still need to see the original. We don't know when or how they plan the switch. We shall have to keep tabs on the painting somehow. I don't know yet how we will do that.'

'The best thing I can do is make the arrangement through the broker, the guy that brought the business in,' Sedgewick offered, keen to help.

'Do that. And arrange for us to see the painting as near to the time they plan to leave the country as possible. Let me know as soon as it has been arranged.'

'Yes, I'll get on to Andrew Shaw now,' said Sedgewick.

Sedgewick was as good as his word and arranged for Philip and one of the company's assessors to meet with the clients at the airport just prior to the painting being loaded onto the aircraft. They would examine the painting and confirm that it was the genuine article, without letting the clients know of their suspicions. The intention was to fix a tracking device to the picture. But in any event the company's stamp would be applied.

The painting would then be taken into the freight loading area where, it was assumed, the switch would be made, if indeed that was what was going to happen. Philip was very apprehensive about the whole plan and feared they would be outwitted.

Philip didn't know how practical James' suggestion of tracking the painting had been. That was something he would have to investigate. He was desperately worried about Andi. In a normal kidnapping, the people responsible would have been in touch, asking for the ransom money. But they were not asking for ransom. They had all the reward they needed, in the form of Andi's skill. They could keep her as long as they liked. He thought if he agreed to insure the painting he could ask for Andi to be released, but that would let them know that he knew the painting was a forgery. That wouldn't do. If he was to trap the fraudsters they would have to believe that he was not suspicious.

24

Philip drove into the company car-park and half-heartedly waved to Wayne, the young man that cleaned the company cars, as he made for the door.

'Oh, Mr Harding!' called the young lady at the reception desk, as he entered the foyer. 'A post-card for you. The postman just left it, I had to pay excess postage on it.'

'Oh, thank you, Bernice. Why was that? A post-card, did you say?'

'No stamp, it's addressed for your urgent attention.' She handed the post-card to Philip, who took it and put down his case.

The post-card was in fact a Polaroid photograph of a row of beach-huts with a sandy bay in the background. The message was simple.

Help, I'm here, but I don't know where it is. You must find me, please.
Andi

Philip's blood ran cold as he read and reread the message. What did she mean? She was there but she didn't know where. Presumably she was at the place in the picture, but there was no indication where it was. He didn't recognise it. It could be anywhere. Perhaps someone in the office would be able to identify it. He would get Julie to photocopy it and send it round all the departments. He ran to the lift and pressed the button for the first floor, where his office was.

He was calling Julie almost before he got out of the lift.

'Julie, where are you? I've got an urgent job for you. Drop everything.'

'Oh, Phil – I mean, Mr Harding. What is it? Are you all right?'

'Hello, Julie, sorry, yes, at least I think I might be. You see this photograph? I want copies made and sent round all the departments. I have to know where this is. Andi is being held there.'

'Oh, let me see – oh, it could be anywhere, but I guess someone will be able to identify it – if they've been there on holiday perhaps. I'll get on to it straight away.'

An hour later, Philip called Julie. 'Any news yet?'

'Nobody has responded I'm afraid. I made it clear it was urgent.'

'Someone must know where it is. Phone all the departments and ask again.'

Fifteen minutes later, Julie reported to Philip that nobody had been able to identify the photograph.

'We'll have to ask head office as well. Can you e-mail the picture to them and say it is imperative that we identify this location. Tell them there's a reward for the person that identifies it.'

'Very well, Philip.' Julie took the original photograph and scanned it onto her computer before attaching it to an e-mail.

Philip was pacing like a caged wild animal, getting more and more agitated. Because he had to do something, he decided to go to Head Office and talk to his boss.

He drove down the A1M on auto-pilot, his mind was elsewhere, but somehow he avoided an accident.

He parked next to the managing director's Rolls Royce. He would never have had the nerve to do that a few months ago. The MD always liked to have at least a car's width either side of his Rolls in case someone bumped it.

He told Maltby what was happening and asked to be excused if he had to rush off in a hurry.

Maltby was pleased to help in any way he could. 'Don't worry about a thing, my boy. I'll make sure things are covered in the office. Would you like me to send Sowerby to Peterborough to take charge in the meantime?'

Philip filled Maltby in on current business in Peterborough and left feeling less anxious about his position. He had been missing from his desk so much lately he had worried about his job.

An hour later, Philip called Julie. 'Any news yet?'

'Nobody has responded I'm afraid. I told them it was urgent.'

25

Several hours later, when Philip returned to his office, he called, 'Any news, Julie?' as he came through the door. Julie came out of her office and the look on her face was enough. Nobody, in either of the branches had recognised the picture on the postcard. Over a hundred people worked in Head Office in London, and there were about thirty people in the Peterborough branch. Surely, thought Philip, someone must know the place. It was almost certainly in England, or possibly Wales. How could it be that out of all those people none of them had had a holiday there? 'Did you send the picture to Harrogate as well?'

'Yes, of course, every branch and every employee has seen it.'

'What can we do now? Who can we ask?'

'The police could circulate the photograph all over the country and they are sure to be able to identify it,' offered Julie.

'Do you think they would do that?' asked Philip. 'They weren't too keen to help me find her before. It was only the possibility of a big money fraud that interested them.'

'No, but now you have proof she has been kidnapped, surely they can't refuse to help,' insisted Julie.

'Yes, you're right. OK, I'll ring them and then I can e-mail the picture. Get me that inspector will you, what was his name?'

'I don't think you told me . . .'

'Never mind, it doesn't matter. Do we know any of the local police at all?'

'Not really, shall I just ask if they would be willing to circulate the picture to help the company? They might be happy to support a local firm.'

'It's worth a try, OK, do that. I'm off home now, but I'll be near a phone. Let me know the minute you hear anything. OK?'

Philip gathered up things from his desk and stuffed them into his briefcase. Then realising he would not be doing any work at home, simply picked up his mobile phone and pulled on his topcoat. He walked over to the window. The Cathedral, lit by the evening sun, looked like an extra-terrestrial craft coming in to land. Had the people who built the cathedral any idea that it would still have a profound influence on the area so many years later. He supposed not. It was like a beacon of hope for Philip.

He was just about to leave when Julie came into his office, excited.

'Oh, I'm glad I caught you, a policeman in Cornwall has just phoned! He knows where the picture was taken! It's a little bay not far from Penzance. I've got a map reference.'

'That's fantastic, Julie, thank you. Have we got a map of Cornwall anywhere?'

'I shouldn't think so, but I'll phone the bookshop and ask if they've got an Ordnance Survey map of the area. I'll do that now, and if they've got one, I'll go and get it. I should just catch them before they close. I just wanted to let you know straight away that we know where she is.'

'That's very good of you, Julie. Then I'll be able to drive down to Cornwall first thing in the morning.'

'Will you go on your own? What about taking Darren with you?' Julie suggested.

'Darren is in hospital, in a coma after being attacked, didn't I tell you?'

'No, you didn't. That's terrible. Is he going to be all right?'

'It's too soon to say. I do hope so.'

The Cathedral was barely visible now the sun had gone down. Julie had been gone ages, what could be keeping her?

'Here we are, Ordnance Survey number 189.' Julie called breathlessly, as she burst into the office, triumphantly waving the map. 'They just had one map of Cornwall and it happened to be the right one.'

They spent a few minutes finding the bay with the map reference provided by the policeman. It was a very remote spot called Pendellen Cove, approached by a maze of narrow lanes, uncoloured on the map.

'You could easily get hopelessly lost down there. They probably thought nobody would ever find them,' said Julie.

'I'm sure that's why they chose it. Thank goodness for our policeman friend. What was his name? I must thank him.'

Philip decided to ask James if he would go with him to Cornwall. James readily agreed and they arranged to meet in Penzance, the nearest place of any size to Pendellen. He drove home and packed a small bag, ready for an early start in the morning. He had estimated the distance from Peterborough to Penzance as about three hundred and fifty miles, which, with a fair wind, would take him between five and six hours. He entered Pendellen into the Satnav and a message came up, 'location not recognised.' Never mind, thought Philip, I have the map.

James' journey was shorter, and he would have the benefit of a motorway for much of the way. He would probably do it in less than four hours. They agreed to meet at a hotel in the centre of Penzance and left it that it would be sometime around mid-day.

Philip enjoyed driving his new Jaguar but as he found travelling back and forward to London easier by train, he had had little opportunity to drive it. This would be the longest journey he had done. He was looking forward to it, especially as he was hoping to be reunited with Andi when he got to Cornwall.

He stopped at the filling station near his home and checked all the car's fluids. He bought bags of sweets and bars of chocolate to keep him going – he didn't plan to stop for a meal on the way.

The route across country to join the M5 was tedious and Philip began to get impatient, but once on the motorway he was able to put his foot down and allow the car to use its performance. All the way as far as junction 31, where he joined the A30, he was able to keep up an average of almost seventy miles an hour. The car, with its automatic gearbox was utterly effortless to drive and Philip felt comfortable and relaxed.

When he drove into the car-park of the Griffon Hotel in Penzance at half past two, he was still not tired and noted with pleasure that the drive had taken only five and a quarter hours, a total distance of 357 miles.

James arrived half an hour later. He was not relaxed. His classic Jensen was showing signs of its age and the worry that the old car might let him down had tired him. He smiled as he entered the hotel, where Philip sat watching the door.

'Hi, James, well done. Good journey?'

'No, not really, masses of traffic and several hold ups. Couldn't really crack on. Still, we're here now. What's the plan?'

'I think something to eat, don't you? I'm starving. The hotel has finished lunches and doesn't start evening meals until seven, so we'll have to go into the town, probably get a bite in a pub, or would you prefer a Chinese?'

'Chinese won't be open yet either, I shouldn't think, and most pubs will have finished doing lunches. Let's just go and see what there is.'

In the end they settled for a burger and chips in a little café just off the main street. It was adequate and the two men felt better for it and able to think about their next step.

'It's getting on for four o'clock, James, should we carry on down to the bay where we think Andi posted the card, or make an early start in the morning?' Philip asked, as he finished his coffee.

'I haven't been able to find a large-scale map of the area, so I've no idea where this place is. Let's have a look at the OS. Is it far from here?' James asked.

'The map is in the car. It doesn't look far from here, that's why I suggested we meet here, but it isn't straightforward. The little lanes that lead to the bay don't go straight for more than a couple yards the whole way. It is a map reader's nightmare. Are you any good with maps? My car has satnav but it didn't recognise the name of the bay. Too small I suppose.'

'Are you suggesting we go in one car?'

'Oh, yes. I can't see any merit in going separately. You really do need someone reading the map to give directions.'

'Oh, OK then, we'll go in yours then, shall we; might as well be comfortable.' James grinned. He liked Philip's car.

'So, what do you think then, leave it until the morning?' persisted Philip.

'Yes, I'm absolutely whacked. Did you book us in?'

'Yes, I did, rooms 23 and 25, on the second floor.'

'Great.'

Although both men were keen to find the little bay where Andi had taken the photograph they were tired and agreed to have a quiet evening to muster their strength. They didn't know what faced them in the morning. They studied the map in Philip's room and when they had worked out the best route to Pendellen, they rested in their rooms until later in the evening when they spent a couple of hours in the hotel bar.

*

26

Andi had been hiding in the beach hut for two days and she began to wonder if her postcard had reached Philip, and if it had, would he be able to identify the location of the cove. Surely, she reasoned, he would come straight away to rescue her. Her store of mouldy bread was almost gone, she had used up all the marmalade and most of the water and she was hungry. She hadn't slept well. The bed was comfortable enough and with the blanket wrapped round her she had been quite warm. The hut was sheltered and well insulated, but the sound of the sea and the seagulls kept her awake. She was also frightened her captors would find her and take her back to the house. She had found the beach huts easily enough so anyone looking for her would find them too. She decided she was no longer safe there. She would have to find another hiding place.

She gathered up her few bits and pieces and the polythene bag with the remaining scrap of bread, and the plastic bottle which still contained a little water, and after peeping out of the door to see if anyone was about, she quietly left and closed the hut door. It was early and still quite dark.

She had not gone more than a few steps along the wooden walkway when she heard a car approaching.

Headlight beams swept the line of huts as the car entered the car park. Philip! He heart thumped with excitement and she began to run towards the steps up to the car-park. But when she heard voices and they were not those of Philip and Darren she froze with fright for a moment. She could not decide what to do – her captors were just a few yards away . . .

The voices were getting nearer. She slid between two huts and found a space under one of them just large enough for her to hide.

Footsteps clattered along the boardwalk.

'Look in all the huts, quickly! She must be here.' Andi recognised the voice; it was Mr Beaumont. The other voice, less distinct, came from further along the walkway. After several minutes during which Andi could hear doors being opened and slammed shut, there were footsteps in the hut above her head. She hardly dared breathe in case she was heard.

'That's the last of them. No sign. Damn her!' shouted the man above her head.

'She must be here, there is nowhere else she could hide. Look again. She is only small, she has probably squeezed in somewhere.'

Noises of doors opening and closing, and furniture being moved roughly about continued for a few more minutes, then all went quiet. Andi began to relax a little. Had they gone? She dared not leave her cramped hiding place in case they were waiting for her to show herself.

It had begun to get lighter before Andi crept cautiously from underneath the hut.

For a moment, Andi thought about going back inside the hut – surely they would not come back – but the hut no longer felt safe, she would have to find somewhere else.

She looked up towards the car-park. It was getting lighter by the minute but there was no sight or sound of anyone. She looked down to the beach. Was that a boat? She hadn't noticed it before, but she could just make out the shape of a small boat, drawn up onto the little beach below. Running now, she made her way down the steps.

The boat was very small, but that was an advantage, anything bigger she would not be able to manage. She checked that there were oars in the boat - it would not be much good without some means of propulsion - and began to pull the little craft down the gently sloping beach.

It was still not light enough to see much of the sea beyond the protecting cliffs of the cove, but there was no sound of crashing waves so judged the sea was not too rough. Once the boat was afloat, she clambered aboard and, using an oar, began to push the boat out further into the breakers that were gently lapping the beach. Driven by fear of recapture, Andi found strength she didn't know she had and soon the little boat was making slow but steady headway into the bay.

Now Andi had time to think about what she was doing. She had been so afraid of recapture that desperate measures were her only option. However, she now realised how serious her situation was. She had no idea where she was, no idea where she was headed, and it began to dawn on her that she had been incredibly foolish to set out on an unknown stretch of coast in winter.

Once beyond the protection of the cliffs Andi became aware of the wind at her back and a much greater movement of the water.

She had rowed a boat a few times when she was in her teens when she and her friends used to go to the boating lake at Nottingham University, so she knew how to propel the boat. This was different, the boating lake had been dead calm. However, although it was uncomfortable, she got the impression that she was making progress. She thought that if she was able to travel along the coast she would eventually find a friendly landfall and, hopefully, help.

Her legs and the bottom of her jeans had got wet while launching the little boat and although the water had not seemed too cold at the time, her legs were now very cold indeed and she had nothing to cover them with. Her coat was thin and despite her exertions, she was shivering. The gentle up and down movement of the sea made her feel nauseous. She stopped rowing and collapsed in a heap, crying.

27

Trying to find Pendellen Cove was, as Philip predicted, a map reader's nightmare, there were no signposts and every little lane looked exactly the same as the one before and the one after. High hedges either side of the road prevented them from seeing the surrounding landscape. They passed several farms which looked like film sets for historical dramas. After about an hour, Philip stopped the car and James confessed to being lost.

'I've just lost count of crossroads and junctions, I don't know which one we have just passed. I thought it was this one,' he pointed to the map, 'but it couldn't have been because the next one would have been a three-lane junction and it isn't, it's another crossroads. How far back was that last farm, do you think?'

'Why?' asked Philip.

'Well, we could go back and ask the way.'

'Do you think that would help? All they will say is – second right, then left, then right, then left again, you can't miss it. That's what locals always say.'

'OK, but at least we can verify where we are on the map and start from there.'

Philip reversed the car to the last crossroads and turned the car to face the way they had come. 'I hope this doesn't turn out to be a wild goose chase, that's all,' he said as he drove back to where they remembered seeing a farm.

'I'm not entirely sure which way we came, this doesn't look right,' said James after a mile or so. 'Oh, wait though, I think I did see that gate. I remember the way the furze had almost completely covered it. Yes, carry on.'

Philip said nothing, but drove on, thinking that all the time they were going the wrong way, they were further from Andi.

When they reached the farm they remembered passing, an elderly man was standing by the entrance with his dog sitting patiently by his side.

'Hello, Gennelmen, lost, are you? Most folks are when they get here. I saw you go by, so I waited for you to come back.'

'Well, yes, I'm afraid we are. We're looking for Pendellen Cove . . . How did you know we would come back?' Philip asked, puzzled.

'Most folks come back to ask for directions – sooner or later. What do you want to go there for anyway? There's nicer places what's easier to find. There's nothing there, not nowadays anyway.'

'No? Well, we'd like to see it nevertheless. Can you direct us?' said Philip, keeping his voice as even as possible despite his irritation.

'Mm, t'aint easy. You'd better not have started from here really,' said the farmer. 'Still, now you're here, I guess you'll have to start from here. Right, have you got a map?'

'Yes, of course,' said James waving the map at the farmer.

'That's half your problem, the map ain't no good for finding Pendellen.'

'What do you mean?' asked Philip, getting cross.

'Well, you see, the lanes all look the same to someone from the city, like you gents. Now what you got to do is keep the sun on your left all the time. Every time you comes to a crossroads, as long as the sun is on your left, you's goin' the right way. Course, coming back would be t'other way round, or if it were afternoon, cos the sun 'ud be going down then, in the west. Course, if it were dark you'd use the moon, and that would depend . . .' Philip cut him off.

'I think I get the idea, thank you very much indeed. You've been very helpful. Goodbye now.'

'That's all right, I'll see you later.' The aged farmer waved his stick amiably as they drove off.

'What did he mean – he'll see us later?' asked James.

'I hope he meant on the way back, not when we go back to ask again!' Philip managed a laugh, but it was a somewhat strangled sound.

The farmer's advice was good. After another half hour Philip and James caught a glimpse of the sea as they reached the top of a hill. The road fell away quite sharply and at the bottom of a steep hill they could see what looked like a car-park.

'That looks like the place,' said James when Philip stopped the car in the car-park. 'Let's go.'

'Wait! Don't just go rushing off. We've got to be careful. We don't know where Andi is, or even if this really is the right place. Let's do a careful recce,' Philip cautioned.

'I see what you mean. We'll soon know if it is the right place from the photo, though, won't we?'

'Yes, we will, but we don't know where Andi is, or if she is still being held captive. We don't want to be seen if we can help it. I suggest we leave the car out of sight if possible. It is too conspicuous here,' said Philip, carefully reversing the car into the gateway to a field. 'Best not approach the cove directly. We'll try going up that hill a little way. We should be able to see the lie of the land from up there,' Philip pointed to a grassy mound the other side of a wooden fence.

They climbed over the fence and headed up the hill, from where they could see down into the bay. They were on the side of the bay from which Andi's photograph had been taken and they could see the beach huts below them. They stood looking at the scene for a few seconds.

'This is the place, James, no doubt about it,' said Philip.

'Yes, looks like it, so now what? Can you see a house anywhere that she might be? It might be worth looking in the huts to begin with and take it from there.'

'You think she might be in one of the huts?'

'Well, no, not really, but it's a start. She might just have left us a clue somewhere.'

They slid down the grassy slope to the walkway leading to the huts. There was not a soul about. The huts looked in poor condition, as if they hadn't been used for some time.

James was trying the doors of the huts with Philip bringing up the rear. A shout from James made Philip hurry.

'What is it? Have you found something?'

'Someone has been in this one recently – look there's a mug that's had tea or coffee in it, and it's still wet. Any more than a day or two and it would have dried up.'

'Oh yes, so it would; you should have been a detective! But we don't know that it was Andi. And if it was, it doesn't help us. We don't know where she is now.'

Since receiving the post card Philip had been thinking that once they found the place they would find Andi waiting. Now, he realised, it was not going to be that simple.

'I just have a feeling she was here. Someone has slept on that bed recently, too. Surely she would have left a note or something to tell us where she is,' said James.

'I don't understand how come she was able to send the photograph and sleep in here, I mean, did she escape from the villains and finish up here? And if so, where is she now. Do you think they might have found her and taken her back to wherever it is they had her held prisoner?'

'Why don't we just wait here for a while, think what we're going to do. She might have just popped out for a few minutes. She'll be back, I'm sure of it.' James suggested.

'I don't know. It doesn't seem likely that she would just pop out, as you put it. Look, you stay here if you like. I'm going to have a good look around the area. See if there are any houses nearby. I'm not convinced she was here. Oh, yes I know she took the photo of the bay, but that doesn't mean she was in the hut does it?'

Philip left James sitting on the bed, holding the empty mug. He walked to the end of the row of huts and stood for a moment looking at the sea. It was a beautiful spot, but the circumstances made Philip feel very uncomfortable. He turned and walked back up the steps towards the car park. Judging from the tyre tracks in the sandy surface of the car park, it hadn't seen much activity recently although there was one set that looked quite fresh.

The only other way out of the car park, apart from the way they had come, was little more than a track, barely wide enough for a car, with grass growing in the middle. It seemed unlikely that there would be anywhere that Andi might have been held prisoner.

Philip walked back the way they had come for several hundred yards. There were no gaps in the high hedges either side of the lane, and when he tried to climb up to look over, he was so scratched by brambles that he gave up. A narrow gap in the hedge, so overgrown that it would have been almost impossible to see from a car unless you knew it was there, opened into a driveway. Philip cautiously entered and followed the curving tree lined drive until he saw a substantial looking house of 1930s design. There didn't seem to be anyone about, but nevertheless he kept well to one side where he would be partly hidden by the overgrown shrubs should anyone happen to look out of a window. He had no way of knowing if Andi was in the house and he could think of no way of finding out. When he was within ten yards of the front door he crouched down behind a large rhododendron bush, meaning to watch for any movements.

The house remained obstinately quiet and after a while Philip decided it was most likely not the place where Andi had been held. Still cautious, he began to creep back up the drive towards the road.

Just as he was about to emerge from the overgrown entrance a large car came into view and without slowing very much, turned into the drive. Philip was only just able to avoid being mown down as he pushed himself into the foliage. The car stopped a few yards from the front door of the house and two men got out. Philip could hear what they were saying.

'Well, I say we go down to the beach again and have a really thorough search. She's not on the road, that's certain and there's nowhere else she could be. She'll be cold and hungry and sure to show herself before long.'

'If you say so, boss. After we get some lunch.'

'No, we go now. We can't waste any more time.'

Philip had all the evidence he needed. These were the men who had abducted Andi and forced her to make forgeries. He would call the police and get them to come and arrest the men. But first he had to warn James, who was still in one of the beach huts where the two villains were headed.

He quickly slid out of his hiding place and ran down the road towards the cove.

'James! Where are you?' he called as soon as he was within earshot.

'What? Have you found her?' said James emerging from the hut.

'No, we need to get away from here, quick, I'll explain on the way. Let's go back to the car. We're about to be found by the villains.'

Walking as quickly as they could up the steep hill was harder than coming down, and by the time they reached the car they were both out of breath.

'Now what?' said James.

'We watch. We can see the approach to the huts from here and you'll see the villains we're up against.'

'Why? How do you know they are coming this way?'

'Because I heard them. I was hiding in the front garden of the house when they arrived. They are looking for Andi as well.'

'So we know she got away then, but where did she go?'

'That, my friend, is the question. Shush a minute, here they come.'

They watched the two men pause to look around before going down the steps onto the walkway in front of the huts. They began to search the huts systematically, and, judging from the noise they were making, doing a thorough job. Philip and James had not been able to hear what was being said until one of them shouted.

'Look at this! Somebody's been here since we were here earlier, she's still about somewhere!' The man came out of the hut brandishing a mug and calling to the other man. 'I left this on the shelf when I searched before, and now it was on the bed. She's been back I tell you!'

'That was me, I moved the mug - I showed it to you, remember,' whispered James. 'They think she's near.'

'She may well be, but we don't know where. One thing is certain, though. We have to find her first.'

After several more minutes of crashing about in and around the huts, the two men left.

28

'One thing is certain, she was here. Those guys said they had searched the road, so she couldn't have gone that way, so what is left?' Philip looked at James for inspiration.

'The sea?' James mused.

'I suppose if there was a boat she might have tried to get away that way. Do you think it's likely? I don't know if she has any experience of boats?'

'We need to get down onto the beach to see if there's any evidence of a boat being kept there, but we can't risk bumping into those two men; we should wait here until they've gone.'

The two men sat in silence until the men had gone.

'I'm glad we thought to hide the car in this gateway. It might have been difficult explaining what we're doing here if those guys had seen us,' said Philip.

'So, now what?' asked James.

'Have another look round down by the huts and on the beach.'

Despite feeling it was a waste of time, they searched the huts again, spending most time in the hut that James felt sure Andi had occupied. But there was nothing. They searched under the huts and when they found disturbed sand under one hut James said it was where someone had hidden. Philip was not convinced.

'Look, if you think she may have taken a boat, let's look down on the beach. There may be clues there,' Philip suggested.

As they were making their way down the rickety wooden steps to the beach, they met a man coming up.

'Oh! Oo are you? What you doing yer?' exclaimed the man. He was dressed in fishermen's blue, with a battered peaked cap hiding most of his untidy mop of grey hair. Philip guessed him to be in his late sixties.

'Good evening to you, too,' said James.

'Sorry, I don't see nobody down yer nowadays, it were a shock, like,'

'That's OK, we're just exploring,' offered Philip, by way of explanation.

'Ere!' began the man as if he had just remembered something, 'you ain't seen my boat 'ave yer?'

'Your boat?' said James.

'My boat, I leave 'er on the beach. Quite safe usually, cos nobody comes yer now, like I said. But er's gone. Some bugger's took 'er.'

James and Philip looked at each other.

'When was this? I mean when was the boat taken?' asked Philip.

'Must 'ave been last night or this mornin'. She were there yes'day.'

Wondering whether to take the old man into their confidence, Philip looked to James for help. James guessed Philip's concern.

'We might know what happened to your boat . . .' James began.

'You ain't took 'er 'ave you?'

'No, but we might know who has. Listen, this is very important.' Philip and James, taking turns with the details, explained to the old man what had been happening, leaving out some parts of the story.'

The old man, he told them his name was Tewdar, was intrigued, and even though he was annoyed at the loss of his boat, he seemed keen to help.

'If the young lady took off last night, or early this morning, she'll not have got far, not unless she's a 'lympic rower, anyhow,' Tewdar laughed. 'It weren't rough last night but it's heavy going in a little boat if you ain't used to it.'

'So, what do you suggest?' asked Philip, eagerly.

'Course, we don't know which way she would have headed, but it would have been easier going with the wind behind her, so, let's see,' he paused, looking to the sky, 'yes, the wind were going westerly yes'day, weren't it? So in that case she'll be on 'er way to Penzance.'

'How far is it to Penzance?' asked Darren.

'By sea, or by road?'

'Both, I suppose,' James suggested.

'Well, by sea, that'ud be about ten miles. I don't know about road, further though.'

'So, even if she didn't set off until this morning – when did you notice your boat had gone?'

'Just now, when I sees you coming down the steps, I'd just come up from the beach.'

'Doesn't help much does it? But at any rate, she might have reached habitation of some sort by now.'

'Oh, yes, unless she's been carried out to sea by a current.' ventured Tewdar, with a wry smile.

'Oh, don't!' said Philip. 'Is that possible?'

'Yes, I would say so, if er ain't a strong rower.'

'Right, well we need to check if she's landed somewhere, and if not we'll need a boat. Have you got another boat, Tewdar?' Philip asked, turning to the old man.

'No, I 'aven't, nuther boat indeed, and get that pinched an all. No – mind,' he said, scratching his unshaven chin, 'I might be able to borrow one.'

'How are we going to do this, James? If I take the car and try places along the coast, you can go with Tewdar in the boat. What do you say, Tewdar?'

'Good plan, yes. So, where is this boat, Tewdar? Darren turned again to the old man.

''Er's in Mullion, I 'ave a friend there what'll lend me a boat. If 'er ain't out fishing that is.'

'And you think he'll let us borrow his boat?'

''Im be a 'er 'e be. 'er name's Edna. Er does a bit of fishing.'

'OK, so how do we get to Mullion?'

'In me boat, if it were 'ere! You'll 'ave to take me in your car.'

'Come on then,' said Philip, 'let's waste no more time.'

'I'll get in the back,' offered James, as he opened the passenger door and folded the seat forward. It was a struggle to get into the rear seat, and he had to sit sideways. 'I don't know why they even bother to put seats in the back, you can't sit in them,' grumbled James, trying to get comfortable.

Tewdar sat in the passenger seat and exclaimed at the comfort of the car. 'This ere's a beauty ain't it? I thought you was a gennelman when I sees you.'

It didn't take long to reach Mullion with Tewdar giving directions. They drove down to the car park near the harbour. After wishing Philip good luck as he set off back the way they had come in the car, James and Tewdar set off immediately down to the harbour where Edna's boat was moored. They reckoned they still had an hour or two before it got too dark.

Tewdar's friend, Edna, turned out to be a lady of mature years, dressed in fishermen's blue like Tewdar, with a long pigtail coiled around her head. She was intrigued by the story of Andi's kidnap and subsequent escape and was happy to lend her boat. She insisted in going with James and Tewdar to help in the search.

Edna's fishing boat was equipped with a powerful motor than gave it a good turn of speed. They headed westwards across St. Michael's Bay. Edna took the boat out about half a mile out to give themselves as wide a view as possible of the bay. St. Michael's Mount was just visible in the distance.

'The chances of seeing a rowing boat in this light are pretty much zero, you understand,' observed Edna, as she steered to boat in the general direction of Penzance.

'Yes, I suppose, so, but we have to try. The young woman is probably frightened and certainly cold.'

'Er's going to be cold, that's for sure, I ain't too warm meself,' said Tewdar.

Edna seemed to know what she was doing, she was steering the boat in wide zigzags in order to cover as big an area as possible at the same time sweeping the area with her powerful spotlight. There were no other boats to be seen. It was beginning to get dark, and soon it would be impossible to search any more.

'What's that?' shouted James, pointing, 'There's a boat on the beach. Can't see anyone with it. Slow down Edna, shine the spotlight.'

Edna shone the spotlight at the little boat, resting on its side on the beach.

Edna took the boat in as close as he could and Tewdar jumped out and waded ashore.

'It's my boat!' Tewdar shouted, see the name – I called 'er Flossy, don't know why, it seemed right at the time. No sign of the young lady,' he shouted as he jumped in to the surf.

The implications of the empty boat quickly dawned on the searchers.

'Hold the boat as close to shore as you can,' urged James, 'I'm going to join Tewdar,' and with that he jumped into the shallow water.

'It looks very much as if she has perished,' said James, looking at the abandoned boat, and although he had never even met Andi, he felt a sharp sense of loss.

'Looks that way. The oars 'ave gone, she probly fell asleep and lost 'em, she would 'ave no chance then,' offered Tewdar.

'Best see if we can take it in tow, I don't know how we're going to tell Philip.'

Between them, Tewdar and James managed to drag the little boat down the beach far enough to tie her on to Edna's boat, and they set off back to Mevagissy.

29

Meanwhile Philip had opted to search possible places where Andi might have come ashore. There were several small villages between Pendellen and Penzance, where he and James had agreed to meet.

Hoping that Andi might have come ashore fairly soon after leaving Pendellen, Philip asked at the Hazephron Inn at Gunwallow first, but nobody there had seen Andi. He tried at Trelawny House holiday apartments, but they were all empty. The village hall at Gunwallow was closed. He called at Clies Farm at Mickleham, but Andi had not called there.

By this time, it was almost dark and navigating the narrow lanes became very difficult.

He drove on and asked at the little collection of houses at Rinsey, near the old Wheal Prosper tin mine, thinking she may have come ashore at Rinsey cove, but she had not called there.

James' phone was either switched off, out of range, or there was no signal. Either way, Philip could not get an answer. He decided to press on, stopping briefly to ask some people taking a late constitutional at Praa Sands. It was useless. He decided to go to Penzance where he had arranged to meet James.

Next morning, James, who had been brought to Penzance in Edna's battered pick-up truck, wasted no time finding Philip, dreading having to tell him about the abandoned boat.

'What? Do you mean she's drowned? Oh, James, the poor girl, desperate to get away, she risked her life, and now she's dead!' Philip looked at his friend, his grief-stricken face grey. He slumped in his seat as the reality of the situation sank in. After a few minutes he looked up, tears in his eyes.

'I'll kill those bastards, they are responsible for Andi's death and they'll pay for it.'

'Don't you think we should now inform the police,' suggested James, tentatively.

'What? The police, yes, we should, especially now there's been a death. We couldn't before, you realise that?'

'Yes, of course, but there's not a lot we can do ourselves, we might have been able to rescue Andi had she still been in the house, but now . . .'

'I'm going to have to tell Darren,' said Philip getting up and looking unseeing out of the window.

'Have you heard how he is?'

'No, I should phone, poor fellow must think I've abandoned him. And when he hears about Andi, he'll be devastated. He loved that girl – not in the same way I loved her of course, he's gay, you know, but he idolised her.'

'So, contact the police then, and the coastguard again, I suppose,' suggested James.

'She could be quite safe in somebody's house somewhere along the coast and they haven't told the authorities,' Philip suddenly brightened, 'couldn't she? Let's not give up hope just yet.'

'That's the spirit, yes, of course, she may have been picked up by a fishing boat or something.'

'Well, we know mobile phones don't work down here, but landlines do, so why hasn't she been reported found by somebody?'

'Could even have been a foreigner. She might be injured, or unable to tell her story, do you think . . .'

'That is a real possibility, hold on to that thought,' said Philip, looking up at James with something like a smile.

'I don't want to think of the alternative, Phil, old man, but I think we have to,' James whispered.

'Don't do that!' Philip snapped. 'She's OK – somewhere. James. I'm sorry, I'm going to have to call my office, just make sure everything is ticking over without me. I'll use the hotel phone in the lobby.'

'Hello, Harding here, put me through to my secretary please,' Philip said when the receptionist answered the phone.

*

While Philip and James were in Cornwall, Darren was making progress. He was sitting up and asking questions. Did anyone know any news of Andi?

None of the hospital staff knew who Andi was. Darren had been brought in unconscious. His friend had given them a name, but he didn't know how Darren had sustained his injuries.

Philip was dreading having to tell Darren what had happened. He drove down to London and was delighted to find him well on the way to recovery. He tried to skate round the inevitable but eventually had to tell Darren about the abandoned boat and fears that Andi may have perished.

'You're not telling me Andi's dead? My lovely Andi, no! She can't be.' He grabbed Philp's arm and tried to hug him. You say there might be a chance she's been picked up?'

'Well, there is a slim chance, Darren, but we have to be realistic.'

'I don't believe she's dead, I would know, I would feel it.'

'What are you going to do, Philip?' Darren clung to Philip's arm, desperately clinging on to the possibility of Andi's survival.

'James has been helping me while you've been ill,' began Philip.

Darren had to think for a moment. 'Oh yes, him with the fancy name.'

'That's him. Turned out to be a really great guy and an enormous help. I could not have coped without him while you've been in hospital.'

Darren was still not well enough to be released from hospital, but he was anxious to be included in solving the forgery business. Philip and Darren were now able to consider what action to take against the fraudsters.

Philip explained that he had to get back to his office to catch up with business having been away for a while. He still had the problem of the insurance fraud to deal with, but he promised to get back to Darren as soon as possible.

30

Beaumont and his cronies returned to the house to discuss their plans.

'Well we have to find her, I tell you. We can't risk her telling her story to the police. We would all be guilty not only of art and insurance fraud, but kidnapping, and you know what that would mean.' Beaumont argued when the man Andi called Bernie suggested they let her go. After all, he said, she had finished the painting.

'Couldn't we just forget the insurance thing . . .' began Reg, the erstwhile cook.

'No, certainly not, I've put a lot of work in to this and we will finish it. There would still be the kidnap thing even if we dropped the scam. No, and you had better come along with me, both of you, because you can't manage without me. We find Miss Pertell and bring her back to the house. If necessary we hide her until the insurance thing is over, then we carry on as planned and get out of the country.'

The two men looked at each other. Neither had been major criminals before teaming up with Charles Beaumont. It had seemed like a good idea to work with a career villain at the time. The rewards offered were more than they had ever dreamed of. Just looking after a young lady in a remote corner of Cornwall had seemed like a doddle. It didn't any more.

'So, what's the plan, Guv?' Reg asked,

'I've told you not to call me, 'Guv'. Keep it formal. Mr Beaumont is my name. OK, I'll tell you what we're going to do. A friend of mine has a boat moored at Mullion, in fact I have been thinking of buying it. We'll get him to take us out and search for Miss Pertell. She can't have got far. We find her and bring her back here.'

'Won't it be a bit like looking for a needle in a haystack, Guv, sorry, I mean, Mr Beaumont,' said Reg.

'Possibly, but we have to find her. Get your coats, it's going to be cold out there. Bring the car round.'

*

After losing her oars when she fell asleep, Andi had been drifting helplessly. All the shores had seemed to be impenetrable cliffs and she had despaired of being rescued.

She was so tired she was barely aware of the cold, but she felt ill and feared for her life. She still could not see any sign of life. If she was not able to get ashore soon, she knew she would die. This stretch of coast was evidently devoid of human settlement. She had no idea how far she had travelled, most likely not far at all. Nor did she know how long she had been rowing. The sea was getting choppy. The movement became more alarming. Her hands were sore, but at least she didn't have to row any more, she was wet, hungry and thirsty. She was convinced she would die before anyone found her.

She slept for a while, and when she woke the sea was a little calmer, but she still felt wretched. It was getting darker again, could she have been at sea for a whole day? She was desperately cold, hungry and thirsty. The meagre remnants of her food and water had long ago been consumed, and subsequently regurgitated and spewed into the sea. It could not be long before she succumbed to hypothermia, if indeed she had not already. She slept again and when she woke she didn't feel cold anymore. She dozed on and off, hardly aware of her situation. A seagull landed on the boat and she reached out to touch it, but it pecked her hand. She didn't feel it. 'Naughty bird', she whispered, before falling asleep again.

She didn't wake even when the little boat bumped ashore on a lonely beach, just as it was getting light. Andi lay unconscious in the boat as it was gradually pushed further up the beach by the gentle tide.

At first light, Andrew Pencreek was beachcombing, as was his wont. He had seen the boat at the far end of the beach as he descended the treacherous steps from the cliff top. He was in no hurry to investigate, boats and bits of wreckage were washed ashore from time to time, he would look at it after he had scoured the beach for treasures in the form of driftwood or interesting shells – anything that he could make into saleable items to tempt the tourists.

He walked very slowly, so as not to miss anything that had been washed up, so it was a little while before he finally came upon the rowing boat.

The bundle of rags in the bottom of the boat didn't look worth investigating, but then he spotted a foot.

'My God! A body! Oh, Lord, what should I do?' he exclaimed. He leaned in to look more closely at the pathetic form and cautiously pulled a fragment of cloth from where he guessed the face would be.

'Oh, Dear God, it's a young woman, she looks so peaceful, what a tragedy!'

But then as the old man was wondering what he should do, he thought he saw a movement in the body.

'Oh, could she still be alive?' Andrew touched the girl's bare arm and felt for a pulse. 'She is,' he breathed, 'she's still alive, but not for much longer unless I can get help.'

Help of any kind was far away, back up those fearful steps and along the road about a mile to the nearest house, where he could call for an ambulance.

Realising that he had to do his best to save the girl, the old man tipped the boat on to its side, allowing Andi's limp body to roll on to the sand. He tried to sit her up, but she was like a rag doll. He took off his coat and, unable to get her arms in the sleeves, wrapped it round the girl as best he could. The upturned boat would protect her from the wind, but the beach itself was cold. Looking back along the beach at the steps, he wondered if he could possibly carry her to safety.

He had been strong when he was younger, but now, in his seventies, arthritis had taken its toll and his strength had been sapped. He feared he would not be able to carry the girl to safety; however, he must try. It was no good leaving her here while he went for help, she would surely die, so he put his arm around the slim shoulders and tentatively lifted. She was not heavy. His other arm slid under her knees and with a great effort he was able to stand with the girl in his arms. His daily treks along lonely beaches in search of little treasures had kept him reasonably fit but whether he could carry the young woman up those dreadful steps he was not sure, but it would not be for want of trying if he failed. Leaving his few bits of jetsam where they fell, Andrew Pencreek set off along the beach with his precious burden.

On the flat hard sand, he managed quite well, taking measured steps as he made his way along the beach.

The steps, cut into the rock hundreds of years ago for some unknown purpose, were only known by a few people now, and the beach was generally thought of as inaccessible.

Andrew had to stop after each step. He looked up at the uneven steps and despaired of being able to make it to the top. Adjusting his grip on the young woman's limp body, he climbed another step, and another. 'Just take them one step at a time,' he said to himself. 'Don't think about how many there are.'

Eventually, he did make it to the top. He was out of breath, panting and sweating. His arms ached, his back ached and the pain in his knees made his eyes water. He gently laid Andi's body down on the soft grass of the cliff top while he recovered. The young woman was still unconscious but seemed to be breathing steadily.

When he had recovered sufficiently to carry on, Andrew once more lifted Andi and began to walk to the nearest house, a distance still of almost a mile.

When he knocked on the door of the isolated house, Andrew was all in. He had let Andi down and propped her against the wall, so that when the householder opened the door, he thought he was confronted by a tramp, and was about to close the door again, but then he saw the body.

With considerable difficulty, still gasping for breath, Andrew explained what had happened and between them they carried Andi into the house and laid her on a couch near the fire.

'I'll get on the phone, there are some blankets in that chest, cover her up and keep an eye on her.'

The owner of the house, a man in his sixties who had chosen to live in this remote place because he didn't like company, now found himself host to two desperate souls, one clearly near death and the other not far behind. He quickly leafed through the telephone directory before realising that the obvious number to call was 999.

'While we wait for the ambulance, I'd better get you a drink, you look as if you need one; I'm Ben Hawley, what's your name?'

'Andrew Pencreek, good to meet you,' muttered Andrew, still gasping for breath. 'Yes, a drink, please.'

'Do you want whisky or something hot?'

'Much as I would like a whisky, I think a cup of strong sweet tea would be better for me, thank you.'

Ben hurried away to the kitchen, leaving Andrew to watch Andi.

When he returned, with a tray of cups and a large brown teapot, Ben was smiling. 'Do you know, I haven't made tea for anyone for years, how do you like it?'

'Strong and sweet, please.'

'Shall I put a drop of whisky in it?'

'That would be nice, thank you'

The two men sat facing each other beside the fire, with the still unconscious young woman on the couch between them. 'So, tell me what happened?' asked Ben.

When the ambulance arrived, the crew quickly assessed Andi's condition and monitored her vital signs. She was still unconscious, but her temperature was just above a lethal chill. Andrew had done the right thing, wrapping her up and treating her as gently as he could. His own body warmth as he carried her up from the beach had probably been crucial to her survival. If she had stayed in the boat for very much longer, she would certainly have died.

'You've saved the young lady's life, sir. Well done,' said the ambulance man as they got ready to take Andi on the ambulance. 'You'd better come along, so you can explain what happened.'

'Oh, I don't know – where are you taking her?'

'Helston.'

'How will I get back?' Andrew asked anxiously.

'I expect transport can be arranged, don't worry. The police will probably want a statement.'

'Police? Why, I've done nothing wrong.'

'Far from it! No, you are a hero. Come on, you'll be all right.'

31

Before going back to Peterborough, Philip met with his boss, Mr. Maltby and told him the story so far and of his intention to pursue the fraudsters. Mr Maltby was sympathetic and encouraged Philip to do what he could. However, he was not as keen for Philip to involve Sedgewick, who had let the company down badly with his involvement with the crooks.

'I've suspended Sedgewick, as you know, Philip, and involving him might give the impression that all is forgiven. I see that he could give you useful information about these people, but I don't want him to be seen to be working with us on this.'

'I hadn't seen this as a company operation, David. On behalf of the company, yes, of course, but not just us. Many genuine art lovers and collectors are being swindled, and I would like to be able to put a stop to it. But I want my efforts to be incognito. It would best if I was not working on behalf of the company.'

'Yes, I see what you mean. Right oh, boy, you do what you need to do. I will help in any way I can, of course. Is that young fellow, Darren helping you?'

'Yes, he is, he feels very strongly about it. And I have a new ally, the man I told you about who was unwittingly involved in the scam. Mr Trentham-Fielding.

'Oh, yes, I remember. Oh, good. But do be careful, my boy. Don't, well, you know, just take care.'

Maltby, stood up to indicate the meeting was at an end. He shook Philip's hand. 'Best of luck. Keep me posted.'

Sedgewick had been as good as his word and arranged for Philip and Robert Miller, one of the company's assessors, to meet with the clients at the airport just prior to the painting being loaded onto the aircraft. James insisted on going along as he was supposed to be the owner of the painting.

They would examine the painting and confirm that it was the genuine article, without letting the clients know of their suspicions. The intention was to fix a tracking device disguised as the company stamp, to the back of the picture.

The painting would then be taken into the freight loading area where, Philip suspected, the switch would be made, if indeed that was what was going to happen. Philip was very apprehensive about the whole plan and feared they would be outwitted.

The flight was scheduled for eight-thirty on the twenty-second.

Despite the fact that they were all waiting for the phone call, they jumped when it eventually came. Philip grabbed the receiver.

'Yes?'

'Meet us at the south end of Bassingbourn Road, Stanstead Airport, just near the roundabout. We'll be in a blue transit van. In an hour, OK?'

'An hour? We'll do our best. Just one more thing, the premium, we haven't discussed the premium. Hold on a moment, would you?'

'We will have adequate funds for the premium when we meet,' replied the voice before cutting the connection.

'Can we make it to Stanstead in an hour?' Philip wondered.

'It's about sixty miles, it'll be tight, but we should do it in your Jag' suggested Robert.

'Right, bring your gubbins Robert, come on let's go.'

Robert, being the smaller of the two passengers squeezed into the back seat and James sat up front.

As Robert had guessed, it was about sixty miles, sixty-six actually, according to the Jaguar's odometer, and driving faster than he was used to, Philip did it in a minute or two over the hour.

Bassingbourn Road was easy to find and sure enough, just by the roundabout was parked a blue Transit van.

'Robert and I will insist we both have to see the painting. James, you slide over into the driver's seat and be ready to take off as soon as we get back to the car, OK? Have we got the policy documents?'

'Come on then, Robert, let's walk over. Calmly OK?' They began to walk towards the Transit van, Robert carrying the briefcase containing the policy documents and the tracking device which he would affix to the painting.

Philip was feeling very nervous as he walked towards the Transit van, it seemed to him very much like the situation that was often depicted in spy films when the two spies are exchanged at the frontier between the Russian and British sectors of Berlin, and just as the two spies are half way across the border shots rings out and the two men drop dead.

'Good morning gentlemen, I am pleased you have agreed to do this little bit of business for us,' said the smartly dressed young man who seemed to be in charge. His dark blue overcoat was good quality and his white shirt and dark blue tie were in good taste, as were his highly polished shoes. His bleached blond hair let him down a little, thought Philip as he shook the man's hand.

'Good morning, I'm Philip Harding and this is my colleague, Robert Miller. May we see the painting please?'

'Of course, Henry, open the door please.' He gestured to a well-built older man who was similarly dressed and who opened the rear door of the van, indicating that Philip should come around. Philip and Robert walked to the rear of the vehicle. There were several men in the back of the van and one of them took the lid off a wooden packing case to reveal a painting approximately forty inches by fifty. The painting was of a riverside with trees and a bridge. Philip thought it looked similar to other Manet paintings he had seen.

'May I take a closer look please?' asked Robert, moving towards the painting. 'Would you be so good as to take it out of the case?' The painting's guardian looked uncertain, but the blond man, who had not volunteered his name, nodded. When the painting was out of it's case Robert made a show of examining it closely and then turned it over to reveal the backing paper which had a variety of labels attached to it. 'I need to attach the company seal which indicates that we are providing the insurance cover,' explained Robert as he opened his case and took out the self-adhesive label.

'We just need to finalise the agreement by the payment of the premium,' said Philip, stepping nearer. 'We were not clear exactly what cover you required so we have prepared two policies. Firstly, this one, he brandished the document, which covers you against all possibilities for one year, and this one,' he took the other document and lifted it up for the blond man to see, 'which covers the transit of the painting to it's destination only.' I need to know which one you require. And what is the destination?'

'It's going to a museum in New York. What is the premium on the annual policy?'

'Fifty thousand pounds. Payable in instalments.'

'And for the transit only?'

'Twenty thousand. Payable in cash now.'

'Very well,' said the blond man without turning a hair. 'Just a moment. He turned and went to the front of the vehicle and opened the passenger door. Philip could hear a mumbled conversation with an erstwhile unseen member of the Transit team. The blond man returned in a minute or two.

'The transit insurance will suffice; the painting will be covered by the recipients at the other end. How do wish the payment to be made?'

'It will have to made in full before the painting travels.'

'So, cash then, yes?'

'Cash is fine, yes. The painting will be cleared to travel immediately if required.'

The blond man gestured once more to his assistant who produced an aluminium case.

'Twenty thousand,' said the blond man and the older man opened the case and began counting out stacks of notes which he transferred to a leather briefcase and handed it to Philip.

'A receipt please,' said the blond man.

Robert had made his inspection of the painting and fixed the label to the back and he now came to join Philip.

'Robert, make out a receipt for the gentleman please.' Robert took out a receipt book and began to write it.

'What name shall I put on the documents?' asked Robert innocently.

'Leave them blank.'

'I can't do that sir, we need the name for the company records. Otherwise we shan't know who owns the policy,' explained Robert, pen poised.

For the first time the blond man looked less than perfectly confident. He looked towards the front of the vehicle again. 'Just a moment.' He went to the front of the van again to consult with the passenger. When he returned he said, 'Make it out to Percival Trentham-Fielding, the owner of the painting.'

'Very well,' said Robert who completed the receipt and handed it over.

'Thank you, gentlemen, I believe that is our business concluded,' said blond man with a slight nod. Goodbye.'

With that the van doors were closed, and blond man and his older sidekick got into the van and the engine started up almost immediately.

Philip and Robert hurried back to their car and Robert set his tracking equipment to search. They waited until the Transit had traversed the roundabout and then followed at a discreet distance.

'Have you got the signal?' asked Philip anxiously.

'Loud and clear,' said Robert with a smile.

The Transit continued towards the airport buildings where presumably it would park, and the painting would be put onboard an aircraft. They didn't know if one or more of the gang would accompany it on a regular passenger flight or if would go as freight.

'This isn't going to work is it?' mused Philip as they got closer to the terminal buildings.

'Why do you say that, we can keep tabs on the picture wherever it goes', said Robert confidently.

'Only if we are on the aircraft with it. That's the bit that worries me. We clearly can't go on the same flight.'

'What you are forgetting is that they haven't seen me,' offered James, who had been uncharacteristically quiet.

'But we couldn't expect you to go,' began Philip uncertainly, 'it's going to be a risky business and, well, no, I don't think we can let you go James. Thanks anyway.'

'It is the only way we are going to do this you know, Philip,' reasoned James. 'We must have someone on the plane with the painting, and someone to follow it the other end. And,' he said with a wry smile, 'it is my painting after all.'

'But not on your own, it is too risky.'

'What do you suggest then, Philip, because we are going to have to park and follow them into the terminus in a minute and whoever is going to follow them will have to have the tracking gear stowed about his person.'

Philip thought for a moment and then agreed. 'OK then, we'll follow on the next flight and then you can get in touch with us once we get there.'

'Right, lets get this tracking gear sorted then,' said Robert, busying himself with the device.

'Won't that thing make the bell ring when you go through?' asked Philip, pointing to the device Robert was fitting into James' ear.

'It's designed to look like a hearing aid, he won't have any difficulty with it,' explained Robert as they followed as closely as they dared after the Transit had parked in the covered car park.

'Right now listen, James, oh, you do have a passport I hope? Good. Now get as close to them as you can and see which flight they are booked on. Then you are going to have to get on the same plane. Here take some of this money,' he handed James a stack of notes from the money the crooks had just given them. 'Then it's just a matter of keeping tabs on them when they land the other end. We will follow as quickly as possible on the next flight. You'll have to phone us as soon as you know their destination. Then we'll let you know when the next flight is, all being well before you take off.' Philip managed a feeble smile, 'If this works it will be a miracle.'

'OK, understood, here goes then.' James got out of the car and using the tracking device soon located the gang carrying the painting.

Robert saw to the parking of Philip's Jaguar while Philip prepared to get tickets as soon as he heard from James which flight the picture was booked on.

Keeping far enough back to be out of sight of the crooks, Philip and Robert walked along the rows of airline stands in the booking hall, keeping a close eye out for the gang. The last thing they wanted was to be spotted.

They could see James at the far end of the booking hall and watched as he disappeared from view.

'I think he's done it,' ventured Robert, 'come on James, phone!'

Philip's phone rang. 'EOS,' said James, and rang off.

32

'EOS, what's that?' Robert asked.

'Airline that specialises in executive aircraft, I believe,' said Philip as he scanned the desks.

The EOS Airlines was the last desk and by the time they got there all the passengers had been checked in and the smartly uniformed girl was just about to leave.

'Miss, excuse me, could you help us? We were hoping to travel with our friend who has just checked in, but we were delayed.'

'I'm sorry, Sir that flight has just closed. The next one to JFK is at seven this evening. Do you wish to book on that flight sir?'

'Yes please, there are just two of us.'

'You realise this is an all Business Class service sir, that will be seventeen hundred pounds, or we can take dollars if you prefer. Do you have your passports?'

'What time do the flights arrive in New York?'

'This morning's flight will arrive at three twenty-five this afternoon and your flight will get there at two forty-five in the morning on the twenty-third'.

The girl was surprised to be paid in cash, but quickly recovered her composure and explained that if they would like to go through to the EOS lounge, they could have a meal before flying if they wished, and they could use any of the airline's facilities while they were there.

They thanked the girl and followed her through to the beautifully appointed lounge where they found comfortable armchairs and ordered drinks

'How are we going to wait until seven, I'll go scatty,' grumbled Robert, looking at his watch for the umpteenth time since they sat in the lounge.

'We'll go and get a meal shortly, that'll take up a bit of time. In the meantime, why don't you read a magazine or something?' Philip suggested, 'there seems to be a whole range over there, just about every magazine you could think of.'

'OK, do you want one?'

'Yes, get me *Motor Sport*, would you?'

By the time they had finished their second round of drinks and had a superb meal in the restaurant it was already mid afternoon and the prospect of catching up with James became the sole topic of conversation.

They had no idea what they were going to do once they reached the other side of the Atlantic, but they kept their doubts to themselves.

They amused themselves by looking at the brochure describing the airline's 757 aircraft, which although designed to carry over two hundred passengers were fitted out with seats and luxurious amenities for only forty-eight very important travellers.

'This is a bit special isn't it?' ventured Robert who had only previously flown economy.

'It certainly is, and at any other time and in different circumstances I would be enjoying this immensely. Right now though it might just as well be a number nineteen bus,' replied Philip with a wry smile.

The two men were seated comfortably and had been plied with drinks soon after take-off. The aircraft was amazing, neither of them had ever experienced luxury like it and the attention they got from the stewardesses was faultless.

'I wish I could afford to travel like this all the time,' ventured Robert. 'When me and the girlfriend go to Spain we go economy, it's like riding in a cattle truck compared to this'.

'Yes, well don't enjoy yourself too much Robert, we need you to keep sober so that we can follow that painting, assuming James has been able to keep tabs on it,' said Philip, looking anxiously at the third double scotch that Robert was drinking.

'Had you thought what we might do if we are able to keep tabs as you put it, on the crooks?' asked Robert.

'Not really, we shall have to play it by ear.'

'If we are caught and banged up for insurance fraud, shall we go to prison in the UK or in the States?'

'Listen Robert, we are not going to prison. We are not going to be implicated. We have safeguarded ourselves by placing a statement with James' solicitor remember?'

'I remember, but I don't believe it will save us. I just have a nasty feeling about this.'

'Try to get an hour or so of sleep while you can, Robert and stop worrying.' Philip turned to look through the window at the landscape of cloud below them.

After a while the whisky and the comfortable seats had their effect and they dosed.

In what seemed like no time at all the stewardess was announcing their imminent arrival at JFK.

'OK,' said Philip, as they made for the door of the aircraft, 'stick together and watch out for James after we get through immigration. With luck he'll be watching out for us. He doesn't know of course that we are on this flight, but he will be hoping we are.'

James was watching for them and soon they were anxiously listening to his news.

'When we landed I made for the baggage retrieval area as soon as I could, to check what happened to the painting. I guessed there must have been a lot of interference on the tracker because I couldn't get a signal. I would have to rely on watching it come off the plane.' He hesitated, 'I couldn't see the crooks anywhere. I watched as every piece of baggage was collected. I asked the baggage guy and he said he hadn't seen a large case at all.'

'Had you had a signal while you were on the plane?' asked Philip.

'Well no, I hadn't bothered to check it once we were aboard, it couldn't go anywhere could it?'

'Here, let's see the tracker,' demanded Robert, anxious that his device might have failed. James handed over the tiny device and Robert examined it closely.

'Well it is switched on and appears to be OK, but there is definitely no signal.'

'So where is the painting?' asked Philip.

'And where are the crooks?' asked Trevor.

'Do you think they sussed us and worked some sort of switch?' mused Philip.

'I don't see how they could have suspected anything. Perhaps they never did intend the painting to go to the States,' suggested Trevor.

'But they paid for themselves and the painting to go on that expensive flight.'

'Very clever', was all James could say.

'So now what do we do?' they all said, more or less together.

'OK, now let's think this through,' began Philip, 'we saw them board the aircraft didn't we, and we saw the case go through to the baggage area.'

'I'm not sure that that is true actually,' interrupted Robert,' we assumed the case had gone through, and as we saw the crooks go through to the departure lounge, we assumed again that they had boarded. What if they came out of the departure lounge another way and the painting was still waiting to be loaded. Could they intercept it and take it out of the airport.?'

'Once you have been checked in it would be very difficult to get out again except to board an aircraft,' said James, firmly.

'Yes, it would but it is not impossible is it. They could have, oh I don't know, they just didn't get on the aircraft.'

'Didn't you see them on the aeroplane James?'

'Well no, but it has all these cosy little enclosed areas, so I could only see a few of the passengers from where I was sitting.'

'That's right, we wouldn't be able to recognise any more than about half a dozen of the people on our flight,' Robert agreed.

'But once you are in the lounge the only way out is through the tunnel to the plane surely,' mused Philip.

'Suppose one of them feigned illness or something.'

'Let's ask the EOS people, they'll know if people didn't fly and for what reason,' James suggested.

'They will, but if we ask they will want to know their names and we don't know them.'

'Oh shit!'

'Somehow we have got to get a look at the passenger list.'

'How do you propose to do that?'

'We'll get Robert to engage the girl at the EOS desk in conversation and while her attention is distracted I can try to find the passenger list,' suggested Philip.

'How will you know where to look?' protested Robert, who was looking more and more agitated.

'Why don't I just ask the girl straight out. It might work.'

Knowing Robert's way with the ladies they agreed that it was worth a try, they could think of no better plan.

No more than ten minutes later, Robert appeared looking very pleased with himself.

'Well?' asked Philip and James together.

'I told her I was supposed to be meeting these two guys off a flight from the UK and I couldn't remember their names. My boss would kill me if I didn't make contact with them. I said I felt sure I would remember their names if I saw them written down. She was as nice as pie and showed me the list. The trouble was that I didn't recognise the names, I didn't know any of the names except James' of course. I just picked a couple and said thanks very much. But then I had a brainwave. I asked what the chances were of getting a seat at short notice. The girl said normally flights tend to be full but sometimes there is a last-minute cancellation, in fact on that particular flight two passengers had to cancel right at the last minute.'

'Bingo! So they didn't fly, and nor did the painting. What on earth are they up to?'

'How are we going to find out stuck over here?' began Philip, 'We had better get back to UK as soon as possible, not that it is going to help much. The next thing we hear will be the claim for the loss of the painting and the company will be five million quid down the drain. I will get the sack or worse, we could all be implicated in this and I am very worried.'

'But you acted in good faith surely, nobody can say you were trying to defraud the company,' offered Robert, not very confidently.

'The thing is we all did know that something was amiss, and we did nothing to stop it,' Philip wailed.

'But we had to go ahead with the insurance to protect Andi.'

'We have left all the information with your solicitor haven't we James? Surely that will protect us from any complicity charge won't it?' pleaded Philip.

'Well not if they reason that we had it all planned from the start and put the letter with the solicitor to provide us with an alibi. It might work but I wouldn't bet on it.'

'But it was your idea!' exclaimed Philip.

'I know, it seemed a good idea at the time.'

'Look you two, never mind all that now, it isn't helping. Let's think about getting back home. I don't like this place.' Robert was looking very uncomfortable and edgy. They all nodded and made their way to the airline desks to see if they could get a flight back as soon as possible.

The return flight was a bit of a comedown for the travellers. The earliest available scheduled flight to the UK was on an Air Atlanta Boeing to Heathrow and it was certainly not luxurious, and in their anxious state not at all relaxing. They fretted about the way things had gone and failed to reassure each other about the possible outcome.

They agreed reluctantly that they would be able to achieve nothing unless they had some sleep so decided to book into an airport hotel as soon as they arrived at Heathrow and not to meet up until the following morning when they would hopefully feel better and have some ideas.

None of them slept and they didn't feel like eating the excellent breakfast offered by the hotel. They did all drink several cups of coffee before they were able to apply their minds the problem.

'I suggest we retrace our steps, go back to the airport where we saw the crooks get on the plane,' began James.

'We didn't see them get on the plane though,' reminded Trevor.

'Well no, in fact we know that two guys got off the plane, and therein lies the problem. We don't know what happened next. We know the painting was accepted and it disappeared along with the other baggage. Right?'

'Well yes, we are agreed on that much I think,' said Philip nodding.

'And we think it would be difficult to get it off the aircraft,' offered James.

'Well we did think that, but we know now that they cancelled at the last minute. Would they have been able to take the package off the plane? They would surely have to explain why they were not flying.'

'So, we need to get to Stanstead to find out, pronto,' said Robert who had hardly said a word all along.

'How do we get there from here?' asked James, 'the car is at Stanstead.'

'Can we get a flight from here?' asked Philip. 'There must be internal flights, I'll go and ask.' He got up and went out of the dining room leaving James and Robert staring into their cups, unable to think of anything useful to say.

'Right, grab your bags as quick as you can,' shouted Philip as he came running back into the dining room, ten minutes later, 'I'll settle up for us all, meet me out the front, there will be a car waiting to take us to the terminal where we can get a flight on a little five-seater job that's going to Stanstead in twenty minutes, we can get on it if we are quick.'

Aboard the little Piper Seneca half an hour later, Philip explained that the aeroplane was flying to Stanstead to pick up a group of businessmen and as it would otherwise have been empty he had been able to secure a reduced rate.

'So how much are we talking Philip, you seem to be spending money like there was no tomorrow,' muttered James, as he looked around him at the luxuriously appointed aircraft.

'There won't be a tomorrow, for me anyway, if we don't find these crooks. Anyway, I can claim it as a legitimate business expense in the circumstances.'

'If you say so.' James conceded.

'This is the life hey?' said Robert as he craned his neck round to look at the pilot sitting up front. 'I wouldn't mind travelling like this all the time.'

The pilot was talking on the radio and a minute later the engines revved, and the aircraft began to taxi. In no time at all the little aeroplane was airborne and they could see Heathrow laid out below them like a map. As the aircraft gained height they looked out of the windows, all evidently deep in thought. No one spoke.

About half an hour later they were landing at Stanstead and a few minutes later they were in one of the airport lounges discussing their next move.

'OK, now we have to find out if anyone saw the crooks leave the departure lounge and where they went after that,' said Philip.

'I'll go and talk to the girls on the desk, with a bit if luck they will know something,' offered James.

'I'll talk to security,' said Philip, 'I'll show my card and explain that there may be an insurance problem,'

'OK then, I'll just nose around and see what I can suss out,' mumbled Robert, slouching off with his hands in his pockets. James gestured a query to Philip who shrugged and smiled.

'We'll meet back here, don't anyone go out of the building and be back here in an hour even if you haven't had any luck,' shouted James as the other two went off in different directions.

When James arrived back at the meeting place the others were nowhere to be seen, he danced around trying to spot them over the heads of the crowds of people in the airport concourse, then he spotted Philip talking to a security officer and ran over to him.

'Philip! Excuse me a minute,' and to the security man, 'sorry to interrupt, may I just have a word,' Philip excused himself and moved a few feet away to speak to James, who looked as if he was going to burst.

'I spoke to the girls at the desk, they are very nice and helpful, they said that the men who had booked onto the EOS flight had to cancel because one of them was taken ill and they called an ambulance to take him to hospital, but they didn't wait for the ambulance! They went off towards the car park, and wait for this, one of the girls who was going off duty saw them and because she remembered them booking in was surprised they had not taken the flight and when she came on duty again just a few minutes ago mentioned it to the other girls. They were talking about it when I went up to the desk. The girl, Alyson is her name by the way,' he paused to smile, 'knows one of the baggage handlers and had asked him if he knew what was going on and he said there had been a security panic when two guys got off the plane.' James stopped for breath and beamed at Philip who was trying to take it all in.

'But we still don't know where they went or if they took the painting.'

'But that's the thing,' breathed James, 'we do! Alyson's boyfriend, yes, she has a boyfriend unfortunately, is a limo driver and he drove the guys to an address in Cambridge.'

'Where is the boyfriend now?'

'Well he phoned a little while ago to say he would be back about seven this evening and arranged to meet Alyson from work.'

'That's fantastic Robert. Really amazing, can you ask Alyson if she can phone the boyfriend and let us talk to him. What's his name by the way?'

'I don't know everything, I was only talking to them for about five minutes!' exclaimed James, who then laughed when he realised Philip was winding him up. He went back towards the counter and just then Robert came back to where Philip was standing.

'I've just been talking to the man that runs the snack bar, oh, I got us some doughnuts by the way,' he said, handing bags to Philip and James. 'I don't know about you two but I'm starving. Anyway, I figured he would know the routine pretty well, he says it is very difficult to get stuff off a plane once it has been loaded and in all probability the package would have stayed on board, but if the passengers who had arranged to fly with the package suddenly decided not to fly, that would alert the security people who would immediately search the plane for bombs and contraband.'

'That's pretty much what the security man told me,' interrupted Philip,' so go on.'

'Yes well, he didn't know what happened in this instance, that was just what would normally happen in those circumstances.'

'Right, so we don't actually know yet whether the painting did stay on the flight. How can we find out? Oh, wait a minute though, James has found out that the men took a limo from the airport to an address in Cambridge, we're going to talk to the driver, he will know if they had a big package with them.

They walked over to the EOS desk and James introduced them to Alyson who was holding a mobile phone.

'You want to speak to Alan?' she said, smiling and holding out the phone.

'Oh thanks, I'll talk to him, shall I?' said Philip as he took the phone.

'Hello, Alan is it, this is Philip Harding, I am a representative of the United and Overseas Insurance Company and we are trying to find some men whom we believe are trying to defraud the company. I understand you took a group of men to an address in Cambridge earlier today? Right, and can you tell me if they had a large parcel or package with them? Oh, they did! What was the address they went to; can you tell me that? Oh well, I do realise that, but in the circumstances... Right, yes, thank you very much, I am indebted to you. Just a sec, let me get a pen. Yes, yes, yes got that, and what time was that? Thank you very much indeed. Oh, one more thing, had they booked the car? They had, thank you so much! I'll pass you back to Alyson now, sorry? No, I don't know Alyson, I have only just met her in fact, she simply answered a question my colleague asked and said she was willing to help us. OK, thanks again, bye.' Philip handed back the phone and smiled, 'you probably gathered what all that was about, he didn't want to tell me the address, customer confidentiality and all that, but he relented, then he wanted to know how I knew Alyson, fair enough I guess. Anyway, I have the address the guys went to, and they did have a package with them when they arrived in Cambridge at about half past two this afternoon. And, the car was booked to take them to Cambridge a week ago! Cambridge next stop I think.' He turned back to the girls at the desk, 'Thank you very much indeed, you have been very helpful. Bye now.'

James and Robert were talking at once and Philip had to shout to get them to shut up.' OK one at a time, now, James, what were you trying to say?'

'I simply wondered if you know Cambridge and would you be able to find the address.'

'That's what I was going to ask,' chipped in Robert. 'Do you intend to challenge them? I mean it would be a bit risky wouldn't it, don't you think we should simply call the police and let them deal with it?'

'Well it would be so difficult to explain; the crooks would probably be long gone before anything was done. I think we're on our own with this,' James ventured.

'No, listen, this is silly,' Philip cautioned, 'What can we do on our own? We don't know how many there are of these villains. We could find ourselves in serious trouble. We have to tell the police – the whole story. Let them sort it out.'

'I guess you're right. Although I would love to have a go at them, the rotters, taking my name and everything,' said James, with a wry smile.

'Right, so if we all agree, lets make sure we know we are all singing from the same hymn sheet, as it were, and get the facts straight before we talk to the police.'

The three men sat down and jotted down everything they knew about the paintings and the kidnapping of Andi and the insurance. Their efforts, once Philip had got everything in order, filled a couple of sides of A4.

'I'll talk to Inspector Wallace in Peterborough,' said Philip, when they agreed the details were correct. 'I have told him some of it already, so it will be easier to fill him in with the rest.'

It took quite a while to relate all they knew to the inspector, but Philip felt sure he could now safely leave it to the police to apprehend the criminals.

'Well, that's that, chaps. There's nothing more we can do now. I suggest we concentrate on finding out what happened to Andi. Any ideas?' Philip looked expectantly at his friends.

33

Andi, meanwhile, was being treated in the little community hospital in Helston.

At first, doctors had diagnosed a simple case of hypothermia caused by prolonged exposure to the cold and wet that Andi had experienced while in the open boat. Closer examination showed extensive bruising, caused, presumably, by severe buffeting in the rough sea. Although she was not badly injured, the time she had spent without food or adequate water had contributed to her condition. She was dehydrated and both mentally and physically traumatised.

Andi had tried to tell the doctors that her friends would be looking for her, but they had urged her not to worry and rest as much as possible. She had been able to tell them her name and a little of what had happened to her.

Satisfied that the police were dealing with the villains, a word they had all begun to use to describe their adversaries, the three men decided to resume their search for Andi.

Philip needed to touch base with his office and Robert thought he should get back to work. James was free and keen to help. Darren, still not well enough to join the search was in regular contact with Philip by phone.

Once Philip had checked that all was well in the office, he joined James once more and they drove down to Penzance, checking in to the hotel they had used before as it was a good base.

'I don't know where to start, James,' said Philip, when they were eating dinner in the hotel restaurant.

'I know what you mean. We have nothing to go by. If, perish the thought, Andi did perish while out at sea, we shall probably never find out, but we have to hope that somehow she got ashore. But if she did, why haven't we heard anything?'

Just then the waiter, a chatty individual, came to see if they wanted sweets or coffee.

'Did you see the evening paper? About the chap that rescued a shipwrecked girl down at Tinker's Cove?'

'What did you say? A girl, rescued from the sea? Tell me more!' almost shouted Philip at the startled waiter.

'It's in the newspaper, I'll get it for you.'

The local newspaper, *The Packet,* had the headline on the front page.

HERO SAVES LIFE OF WOMAN WASHED UP ON BEACH

The article that followed detailed the rescue, emphasising the heroic rescue that involved the elderly hero climbing treacherous steps from the beach carrying the woman to safety.

The 'hero' was a local man known for his beachcombing along the beaches of Mounts Bay.

'It's got to be Andi!' exclaimed Philip when he saw the paper. 'It must be, oh James, that's wonderful.' Tears were running down Philip's face as he clumsily hugged James, who, although he had never even met Andi, was now emotionally involved. He too wiped tears from his eyes. 'It does look like it my friend, we must find out where she was taken.'

It didn't take long for them to phone the local paper and ask for more information. The editor wanted to interview them to add to the story but Philip said he would be happy to fill them in with the details later, but as things were still unresolved, he couldn't say anything at this stage. All he wanted to do now was to find out where Andi had been taken. The editor, with the promise of a good story, was keen to help and told Philip that the girl, they didn't have a name yet, was in the community hospital in Helston.

'The young woman is still very poorly, you understand, so please don't excite her.' The doctor urged as they were led to the single ward of the little hospital.

Flowery curtains concealed the bed, and it was with bated breath that Philip pulled them aside to see the patient.

'Andi?' Philip whispered as he peered at the pale face. The patient stirred and opened her eyes.

'Philip! You found me!' Andi tried to raise her head but could not. A beautiful smile transformed her sickly features and she began to cry. Philip, crying, too, found Andi's hand under the covers and held it to his face.

After a few minutes, Philip turned to James and smiled.

'It is Andi, James, she's going to be all right. Come and see her. James stepped tentatively closer to the bed and smiled at Andi. She smiled back but it had been too much for her and she closed her eyes.

'Leave her now, please,' urged the doctor, who had been hovering nearby. 'Your friend is well on the way to recovery, but she needs a lot of rest. You can come and see her again tomorrow, but please don't stay too long.' He smiled, pleased at the development.

No doubt boosted by the knowledge that Philip was near, Andi's recovery speeded up and within a few more days she was sitting up and demanding to see Philip.

Everything happened quickly. Darren was released from hospital and took the train to Penzance.

News had come through from Inspector Wallace that Beaumont and his cronies had been rounded up in Cambridge and were being charged with kidnap and fraud. The police, although not pleased with Philip for withholding evidence and trying to go it alone, relented and congratulated the friends for their part in catching the criminals.

When Andi was well enough, they
 returned to Peterborough where Andi said she would like to stay permanently.

Philip had a studio built in the grounds of his house and Andi was encouraged to paint her own pictures, never to make a copy again.

Darren and James became frequent visitors to the Harding household in Peterborough.

Watch out for 'MONK'S GOLD'.

Publication expected later in the year.

The author welcomes comments on his books. You can contact him by e-mail. *myklo@hotmail.co.uk*

Lightning Source UK Ltd.
Milton Keynes UK
UKHW012218240519
343285UK00001B/21/P